THE ALTERNATE WORLD

THE ALTERNATE WORLD

by Kathryn Starke

CREATIVE MINDS PUBLICATIONS

Cover Design by David Pfendler

ISBN 979-8-218-51666-6
Library of Congress Control Number: 2024920058

Printed in the United States

Published by Creative Minds Publications
www.creativemindspublications.com

"To thine own self be true."

-Shakespeare

PROLOGUE

People often talk about finding your purpose, identifying your why, and the importance of simply being authentic. Easier said than done. Does any adult remember how it feels to be a teenager? If they do, they can't possibly understand how it feels to be a teenager present-day with everything magnified through the power of social media. Everyone has an image to uphold. So, how do you balance the space between an online presence and your true self?

Ask anyone from the age of thirteen to thirty to ninety-three on any given day about their daily lives and listen to what they say. People often tell you a surface level story. You usually hear about a classmate's brand-new car that they just got for their birthday or your best friend's spring break vacation to the islands. On the surface, they seem appreciative and excited about life. If you listen more carefully or watch closely, their real story will emerge, but you must dig deep, ask questions, and be curious. That classmate happens to be the star basketball player in school who woke up on his sixteenth birthday to find a scribbled note on the breakfast table about his new Lexus SUV in the driveway. His parents were already gone for the day and have yet to attend a game.

Your best friend's adventure to the islands is in fact a trip to her grandmother's house with her mother and three younger siblings as a safe haven since her father has a volatile side and her mom is seeking a divorce. Everyone keeps secrets, either on themselves, family members, or friends. There are countless scenarios. A girl dreams about her crush who never asks her out or the student body president who does not get accepted into his first-choice university. Do we ever really know anyone besides ourselves? Sometimes, we don't even know ourselves.

Outside appearances rarely match the feelings someone has on the inside. Regrets are buried deep. Humans are very good at pretending, no matter how old they may be. How many people are living the life they truly imagined for themselves, and how many people are just keeping up appearances?

If you are really supposed to understand your passion and follow your unique purpose, then what prevents people from achieving their own hopes, dreams, and desires? What if a world existed where people could be their true authentic selves without judgement-where life choices are entirely up to you and what's best for **you.** What are you going to choose to do?

ALTERNATE WORLD

Gina wanders around the mansion greeting the newest members, hugging old friends, and whispering into the ears of the men in tuxedos. The dapper men swiftly deliver food to tables, dust furniture, carry luggage through the main doors, and hang portraits on the enormous hallway wall. Gina effortlessly flits around the gigantic home clearly in charge of everything. She wears a pastel pink gown and moves so gracefully in and out of rooms that it almost looks like she has wings. She often walks into a small room by herself to flip through a large book resting on a podium before she peers into what seems to be a looking glass. She seems to focus on a group of junior high school students in a faraway world.

My World: Chapter One

Our junior high school hosts a ninth grade dance every spring for the graduates before they soar on to high school. Since "college readiness" is of the upmost importance in our community, the rising tenth graders spread their wings and choose one of the many public schools, private schools, Catholic schools, or in my case, a New England boarding school, in preparation of attending college. The dance is one of the last nights we will all be together in the same place; it is a rite of passage for teenagers at Deep Spring Junior High School.

Before the big event, my mom and I visited every department store, independent boutique, and consignment shop to find the perfect dress. Not too many sparkles, no red, (everyone wears red), thick, comfortable straps that won't bother me all night, and, of course, floor length since it is formal. I chose a long hunter green dress complete with matching emerald jewelry and gold stilettos. I'm going with Jonathan, my neighbor who I have known since the second grade; he asked me to go as friends. My girlfriends say he finally got the courage to live out the dream date with his crush and used the friend card as an excuse. Honestly, whatever the reason, it's so nice to have a date without the pressure. Everyone has been talking about who's doing it with who tonight and where the best after parties will be. My night is all planned out. It includes dinner out with friends, dancing, then the after-hours party sponsored at the local community center.

Preparation for the long-awaited day begins at 3 PM with hair and make-up appointments before group photos begin promptly at 5:00 in our neighborhood clubhouse. We all arrive with our parents in tow then pair off with our respected dates. (These details were sorted out weeks ago). We exchange boutonnieres and corsages; mine, of course, being emerald green from Jonathan. We pose for pictures by ourselves, with our designated dates, with our girlfriends, and finally at least ten more shots with the whole crew. We hop in the stretch limos and wave good-bye while blowing kisses out of the roof and windows. Our parents remind us to stay safe and have fun before they turn the clubhouse into their own little party, the real reason for all this fanfare.

Dinner reservations are made at a delicious Italian restaurant; it's the kind of establishment with crisp, white tablecloths, and candles, that serves homemade rosemary bread with dipping oil. It's a favorite spot of mine for special occasions. We pile out of the car through the front door and are immediately escorted to our reserved table in the middle of the restaurant. Annie and her boyfriend sit across from me. Maggie and her boyfriend are seated diagonally across. My best friend Erin is beside me with a guy from her homeroom who asked her to the dance less than a week ago. Ellie and her good friend Rachel also join us for dinner. Ellie has been a friend of mine since sixth grade; she is cute, short, and blonde, but painfully shy. Rachel is the outgoing one in that friendship pair. She is beyond excited tonight because she heard that Kevin, the boy she is obsessed with, is also coming stag.

Often depicted in every school movie, our formal is no exception to the stereotype. We enter the decorated gymnasium to hear the DJ spinning the top forty tracks. Groups of girls are gossiping on one side of the gym with their counterparts casually standing on the opposite end. From the doorway, I see many of our classmates already dancing or socializing (perhaps strategizing) around the punch bowl, which may or may not be spiked at this point. We respectively remain in our twosomes except for Rachel who spots Kevin as soon as he walks in. She hauls ass in his direction after telling Ellie she'll catch up with her later. Ellie ends up hanging with Jonathan and me most of the night, and we didn't see much of Rachel again. Around 10:30, she jumps into our circle.

"You'll never believe this, but Kevin wants me to go

with him! So don't wait for me; I'm sure we'll see you at the after party."

Ellie just stares at her, but it is evident that her mind is racing.

"Are you sure that's a good idea?" I ask Rachel.

"Of course it is! Why wouldn't it be?"

Jonathan pipes in, "Did he tell you where he's going?"

"I assume the after party. I'm just going to ride with him."

"Don't assume anything." Jonathan firmly says.

Rachel hears him and gives a smirk but doesn't respond. She gives Ellie and me a hug before skipping off.

"I'm not so sure about this," I say to Ellie, who is still communicating with only her eyes.

After what seems like no time at all, the DJ strongly suggests that we find that "special someone" for the last dance. Jonathan and I walk toward the dance floor arm in arm.

Miraculously at 11PM, our whole group reunites by the limo to drive down the street for the after party. The center smells of pizza. A tower of water bottles is displayed beside the stacks of pizza. Big screen TVs, casino themed games, and raffle prizes are displayed around the room. This ninth-grade playground is open until 4a.m., just for us. It's around 12:30am when Rachel suddenly appears in the game room.

"Hey guys. How's it going?"

"Rachel, you're here! Did Kevin bring you?" I'm honestly shocked to see her.

"I took an Uber."

"Are you kidding me?"

"You all were right." Her shoulders slouch like a child who had just been reprimanded.

"About what?"

"Kevin's plan was at the hotel instead of here."

"Are you okay?"

"Yea. He said he was just going to go there for a little bit to hang out since he and his buddies had rented some rooms for the night. Once he started drinking and smoking, it was evident he had different plans for the night. When he started popping someone's prescription pills and vaping, I was out. Jonathan was right. I'm just glad I figured it out in time."

"Did he make you drink or smoke?" Jonathan asks.

"He tried to. The more I said no, the angrier he got. I had to leave. You won't believe who else showed up at the hotel. Or maybe you can since none of them are here."

"I bet I can guess." I smugly respond knowing good and well my next-door neighbor was just one of the guys bragging about his personal conquests planned for this weekend.

"Let's just say a good number of our classmates may not even remember tonight. I'm going to grab a slice of pizza."

Our group begins to wind down around 3am, so we climb into the limo a little more disheveled than earlier. I lay my head on Jonathan's shoulder, and Erin's head is resting on my lap on the ride home. The driver makes a few stops in the neighborhood for each of us to arrive home safely. My parents have left the porch lights on and obviously haven't fallen soundly asleep (parents of teenagers get as much sleep as parents of infants in the wee hours of the night). I try my best to tip-toe upstairs to my bedroom when I hear my mom say good night.

"Good night, Mom," I whisper back. I brush my teeth, throw the dress on the floor, and collapse on the top of my bed.

Chapter Two

Monday morning at school is very interesting. I notice some couples seem closer than ever before while others are suddenly not speaking to each other. Everyone is still exhausted and secretly hoping our teachers will either put on a movie or assign us a bunch of busy work to silently complete (anything to avoid a lecture). Some junior high schools plan a teacher workday the Monday after their dance-genius! Our class officers, or maybe the administrators, didn't get the memo. Nevertheless, Erin and I are sitting in the cafeteria this morning when Rachel, who looks more alive than the rest of us, races over to our table.

"Girls! The craziest thing happened to me last night. I thought it was a dream. It felt like a dream. It has to be a dream, but I'm pretty sure it was real."

"What on earth?" Erin starts.

"I was heading to the gas station right after family dinner when my car broke down right there at the intersection of Church Road. You know, the one with the leading green to turn."

"Are you okay?" I interject.

"Yea, you knew that 2010 Audi wouldn't last much longer. My mom loved it though. Anyway, all of a sudden, this lady in a pink dress shows up and just starts pushing my car into the station all by herself while I was still behind the wheel."

"You're kidding? Where did she come from?"

"That's the thing..she just kind of appeared out of nowhere. She told me to leave my car and she would take me home."

"You didn't call your parents?"

"For some reason, I felt at ease with her. Her name was Gina."

"So what happened?"

"I hopped in her little vehicle that was suddenly parked at the station and gave her directions to my house, which I know she heard, but she turned down a windy road instead. She pulled up to a huge house asking me to come in for a sec while she grabbed something. I opened the car door slowly, taking in this whole bizarre situation and followed her up the steps to the front porch and through the double doors. It was like I was in another world just floating around without a care in the world.

"Wait, what street did she turn down? I can't picture."

"I have no idea."

"Weird," Erin and I say simultaneously.

"Oh, I know I sound crazy. I am still confused about the whole thing."

"I believe you, but it definitely sounds like a dream," I add.

"So, whose house was it?" Erin asks.

"I think it's hers. There were some people there too. She told me I was always welcome there, then she drove me back home."

"This doesn't make any sense!"

"I know! That's why I'm still in shock. I haven't told anybody about this, so don't breathe a word, okay?"

"Who are we going to tell?" I ask.

"Who's going to believe us?" Erin adds.

"Good point." Rachel confirms.

Chapter Three

Two weeks later, it is official. I graduate from junior high and will be starting tenth grade at Kerrington Preparatory School in Massachusetts. It is definitely longer than a quick road trip from my friends and family in central Virginia. I have been constantly reminded by my parents, teachers, and guidance counselors that I am very fortunate to be accepted in my top choice of schools. Evidently, the brochure convinced them all that this school provides all students with the opportunity to do amazing things in this great wide world. They also told me more than once, *it's your decision, Eve, and whatever you decide, we will support you.* (I know they were secretly hoping that I chose a closer school). I accepted the scholarship offer to the boarding school much to my parents' dismay; the thought of going to school in New England presented multiple adventures for a girl like me.

I have never really been one to follow the crowd; I didn't drink or party with the "popular" kids, nor did I maintain a perfect 4.0 GPA. I managed, however, to make a connection with all 203 students in my class. I've always kind of felt like I was born in the wrong city (sometimes in the wrong decade), but I have a good feeling about this new path. I am the only one in my class going to the Kerrington, but I am ready to go. Big risk, big reward. I don't plan on anyone or anything getting in my way.

So here it is, two days after graduation. I have finished packing my bag for beach week, a weeklong celebration for classmates (and parents) to head south to the beaches of the Carolinas to celebrate our academic accomplishments and enjoy seven days surrounded by best friends. Five of us are staying in Maggie's beach house (her parents are loaded) in more of a private beach area, so we may not run into any fellow alum at all.

"Beep, Beep!" Maggie's mom pulls in the driveway; Maggie is blaring the radio and hollers out the window, "Eve, you're up front!" I always get the position of shotgun because I'm the only one with any sense of direction. We'd never get anywhere without me even with the assistance of the high-pitched moody woman on the GPS.

"Hi girls!" I say to Maggie and Ellie, who are sitting in the back seat, Ellie's head already buried in a book. She got a scholarship to a small liberal arts school in Ohio and is leaving in three weeks. Maggie is going to the public Blue-Ribbon high school outside of Richmond. She already knows she wants to be a third-grade teacher in our district after she graduates from college.

"Annie is at Erin's house, so once we pick them up, we are on our way," Maggie explains as her mom reverses out of the driveway, quietly listening to everything. Annie is going to the same high school as Maggie, and Erin is going to one of the neighborhood private schools. They are waiting at the front door, bags in hand, when we arrive. We all settle in for long awaited three-hour trip to the Outer Banks.

Maggie's mom starts the conversation.

"Eve and Ellie, when do you all start school? I imagine you will have to start packing soon."

"I leave around August 15th like the college kids," I answer.

"My school doesn't start until after Labor Day," Ellie whispers.

"And do you all have roommates you are matched with at your schools?"

"I know at my school, they use our applications, a questionnaire, and a personality quiz to match us with a good learning partner, the brochure's term for roommate, unless you know someone," I say.

"I cannot imagine getting paired up with a loser or a know-it-all or someone who thinks they're so great!" Maggie interjects. Her mom gives her a look through the rearview mirror, and she stops talking. I, of course, will be paired with a "random" since I have not met a single person who will be starting at Kerrington, and there are about 125 students in the incoming class; not all of them are boarders. These two and a half months of summer are all our group has left together before we start the next chapter in our lives. Come August 15, nothing will ever be the same.

Three hours later, the car arrives at Maggie's beautiful beach house. We grab our luggage and run inside to claim our beds before we immediately change into our bikinis; we have at least two good hours of sunlight left. Maggie's mom is in the kitchen unpacking the groceries she bought. We pack a cooler of water bottles and a beach bag of *People* magazines to take with us.

"Bye, Mrs. Johansen!" we say in unison as we head out the door.

"Bye, girls. Have fun at the beach," she calls back.

The house is only a two-minute walk from the beach. We set up our chairs in a circle close to the ocean, and the dialogue begins again.

"So, Eve," starts Maggie, "are you so psyched about going to New England all by yourself?"

Annie chimes in, "Yea, no parents, boys at night, and real winters, what a life!"

"I don't know about all that, but I'm definitely excited. You all have to come up and visit," I respond.

"When is everybody's fall break?" questions Erin. "We have to plan a night out at home to catch up when everyone is back.

"I don't think I have one since we start later," states Ellie, "but I have a week off for Thanksgiving" she adds reluctantly.

Maggie shouts out, "This is crazy, guys. I'm going to miss everyone so much. We have to make a pact to keep in touch!"

Maggie sounds slightly desperate, and I know it's because she is worried that we will all grow apart. (Only she and Annie will be at the same school next year). While I hope the five of us can get together for dinners in three years and still be the same even though we will all be planning our college journeys by then, I am realistic in knowing that everyone changes, people go in different directions, and that's okay.

The sun begins to set when Maggie announces, "We have dinner reservations at Nelly's at 7pm."

That is our cue to head back to the house to shower and prepare for a nice dinner. I'm starving anyway, so I'm ready to roll. We all get ready quickly, and Mrs. Johansen drives us to the restaurant. At Nelly's, we are seated at a long oval table adorned with white tablecloths, napkins, and wine glasses, which we use for iced water. Maggie takes the seat at the head of the table right beside her mom, who wanted a night out with the girls. The great thing when she comes is that she picks up the tab, and since every entree is at least thirty dollars, I am fine with her being here. She raises her wine glass, filled with Chardonnay, and initiates a toast.

"To my favorite group of girls, may your future always be bright no matter where it takes you!"

"Cheers," we say in unison and clink every single glass at the table.

"And always come home," Mrs. Johansen added with a chuckle.

Chapter Four

Summer flies by even faster than usual this year, and everyone's first day of school is a different date on the calendar. I am leaving about two weeks before the private school begins that Erin will be attending. I'd rather be the one leaving though than having everyone leave me. It is a few days before I'm supposed to move when she calls and asks if she can stop by to say goodbye. She rings the doorbell while she opens the screen door and runs up the stairs to my childhood bedroom like she's done so many times before. We both sit side by side on my bed and just sob; we don't admit it but are keenly aware that we are headed down two completely different paths.

Forty-eight hours later it's time to leave and start my own journey. I say all my good-byes at home to my father and sister since my mom is flying up with me. I pack only two suitcases, one for fall and winter clothes, and one for shoes. We will buy my dorm bedding and bathroom essentials at the Target near campus. After the two-hour direct flight, unbelievably, we take a cab to campus and register at my dorm. My roommate is already settling in and displaying her picture frames when we walk in. She stops what she's doing to greet us.

"Hi, you're Eve right? I'm Jennifer. Nice to meet you."

"Nice to meet you too; this is my mom, Jane Thompson." Mom steps forward to shake hands with Jennifer.

"Hi, Jennifer," Mom says, "This room looks lovely. When did you get here?"

"About 9:30 this morning; I'm from San Diego, so my whole family came up to help."

"That's wonderful," my mom continued and nods approvingly.

Jennifer and I smile at each other; I know we seem excited to be rooming together, but we really have no idea who the other one is and what we are really doing here. Mom stays to help me unpack before we head out for errands and grab a bite to eat before she checks into her hotel. She has to fly back home tomorrow since she's a teacher and her work week starts in two days. I know my mom can't stay here forever, but I don't know if I'm really ready for her to go either. I guess it is better this way, but I know I'm going to lose it when I have to say bye. *What was I thinking again when I decided to move this many miles away?*

After our family members are gone the next day, Jennifer and I are on our own to explore our new home and all it has to offer before classes begin in two days. As "fresh meat" at school, we are instantly sought after while walking around the quad. We are also invited to a house party tonight. Most of the student body are students who live in the area and carpool to school with upper classmen. Like high schools everywhere around the country, there always seems to be a party going on somewhere, and we were just asked to attend our first one here. One of the girls who lives in our building is apparently dating a guy who lives nearby and offered us a ride. We definitely need to go.

We are greeted at the door of someone's house by several tanned guys wearing polo's and double-fisting Miller Lite cans. They offer us each one, and Jennifer accepts. Jennifer and I agree upon entering not to separate, but she forgets that pact as soon as an older 6'2 blonde baseball player catches her eye. I stand by the wooden homemade bar slab observing the room and keeping a close watch on Jennifer. A sandy-haired guy comes up to stand beside me.

"You're new, right?"

"Is it that obvious?" I ask, embarrassed.

"No, it's just I've never seen you before."

"Well, there are about 400 students that go here. How would you possibly know?"

"I'm Matt; this is my house, so I usually know the regulars."

"I'm Eve. What year are you?"

"I'm a second year."

"No way! I'm a first year."

"I know," Matt says with a sly grin.

"Maybe we'll have classes together?"

"Maybe..." he replies, knowing like I do we probably won't.

Jennifer comes staggering over to where we are standing and just hangs on me. What happened to Jennifer? I know we have not been here that long.

"I'm ready to go, Eve. Can we go?"

"Sure," I say, "Nice to meet you, Matt."

"You too, Eve. Goodnight."

"Who's Matt?" Jennifer slurs on our walk back to the dorm. She must have had more than that one beer.

"He's a second year."

"He's cute," Jennifer said.

"I guess. He is nice," I briefly answer with a grin.

We arrive to our dorm room and both pass out on our own beds. If this first night is any indication of boarding school life, I have no idea what to expect, but I know it will be good. The only life I have ever known has been very predictable. This is the reason I chose Kerrington, new people and a much-needed change of pace.

Chapter Five

My first class is creative writing, which is a packed course of all grade levels. I'm sitting toward the back of the lecture hall when Matt walks in, waves at me, and walks up the steps to sit in the chair beside me. I'm shocked.

"Hey Eve! It looks like we will have a class together after all."

Matt and I end up having a debate class together too. After just a few weeks of school, he and I are definitely hitting it off. Jennifer and I have met so many more girls in our building and regularly meet for dinner. It's not home cooking, but there's always a variety of options. On Saturday nights, we usually spend time at Matt's house parties. (I have no idea where his parents are every weekend.) Jennifer is dating one of his teammates, so it works out perfectly for the four of us.

This afternoon, every possible organization or club you can imagine sets up a booth on the lawn with information packets and clipboards to sign up for open house meetings. Jennifer is all about the Kerrynites, the female service organization. You earn points, have socials, and wear special shirts. It reminds me of a college sorority, which is not exactly me. I'm considering running for student government.

Jennifer visits an open house every single night to meet a new organization. I decide to hang up posters everywhere as a candidate for sophomore class vice president. Big risk, big reward, right? After two more crazy weeks pass by, Jennifer is initiated into the Kerrynites, and I am installed as a class officer. We celebrate our accomplishments with dinner out, followed by a night with our favorite boys, Matt and Eric, her official boyfriend as of two months. Our semester remains consumed with classes, meetings, and parties (such a hard life). Midterms seem to arrive out of nowhere.

All of sudden, I am booking my trip back home for fall break to finally hang out with family and friends. It's crazy how your childhood becomes a distant past in just three months. I can't wait to tell Maggie and the girls everything. It is evident that she is too because she leaves me a text message when I'm sitting in Logan International.

Call me when you land. We're all going out tomorrow night! See you soon!

My dad is standing at the bottom of the escalators when

I arrive at the airport back home in central Virginia. It's always just him and the car service people standing there. I don't know if he's aware there is a "reuniting area" upstairs with couches to greet arrivals, but at least I always know where to find him.

"Welcome home, honey. Are you hungry? Mom has dinner ready for us when we get home. Are you eating enough? Are you getting plenty of sleep?"

"Yes, Dad. I'm good. I eat and sleep every day."

"We've missed you, Eve Bee."

I love when my dad calls me that. It's his own special nickname for me.

"I've missed y'all too." Dad grabs the luggage from my hand as he leads me to his car parked in the front row. We then drive twenty minutes home.

"Do you ever hear from Hope? Is she planning on coming home at all? "

"According to your sister, she can't afford to miss a moment at college; I don't think she's even coming home for her fall break this year."

"Is mom okay with that?"

"I think your mother is still hoping for the best."

"That sounds about right," I agree.

When Dad and I walk in the door, Mom is serving our plates with her famous parmesan chicken and rice.

"Eve! Welcome home, darling! Are you hungry? Are you eating enough?"

"Yes, Mom, but I'm excited for this home cooked meal."

"Well, you must fill us in on everything, Madame vice president."

"Mom, we talked just a few days ago."

"You must be hungry."

I nod while chewing her deliciously prepared rice, then continue, "I'm starving actually, but I'm very glad to be home. I wonder if my school is harder than if I stayed home and went to school here."

"I don't know, dear. I would think that all high schools around this area are challenging like yours."

"That's true," Dad interjected, "But you're going to a preparatory school grooming people for Ivy League universities, so I would think it would be more rigorous."

"Well, I'm feeling it."

"Are you happy?" Dad asks.

"So far. I won class vice president, I love my roommate, and I've made a good group of friends. I like it."

"Well, that's good. We just want you to be happy. You know you can always come back home whenever you want."

"Thanks, Mom."

I excuse myself from dinner and drag myself up the stairs to take a shower and get a good night's sleep. It's so calming to sleep in my own bedroom at home and have my parents cook for me. The next morning, Dad is cooking pancakes and eggs, so I run downstairs in my pajamas. It feels like forever ago when this was my daily routine; I do miss it now that I'm here.

I spend the day around the house catching my mom and dad up on all of the details of my new school. When you sleep in until noon, there's not much of the day left. At 5:15, I put on my jeans, tall brown boots, a hunter green top, and my favorite brown leather jacket. Maggie sends me a text at 5:47 that she's on the way, and her mom pulls into the driveway at 6:00 on the dot. We head to a pizza place downtown where her mom drops us off. Maggie turns 16 before me in just 2 months, and we can't wait for that little bit of freedom to arrive. We check in with the perky hostess to put our names on the list to score a table for five. We are standing around the host station watching the door open and close as people fill up the restaurant this particular Saturday night. Annie and Erin walk in the door right when the hostess yells, "Johansen, party of 5?"

"Over here!" Maggie shouts back.

"Right this way," the hostess states like she's reading a script.

"Where's Ellie?" I ask.

"Her mom is dropping her off after Mass, and we're taking her home," Annie replies.

Our server is already waiting at our table while we remove our coats and get comfortable on the stools at the high-top table.

He smiles and says, "I will bring you all some waters while we wait for one more person." We all say thank you in unison.

"I'm so glad we could all get together," I express. After all, it has been almost four months for all of us apart except for Maggie and Annie, who are apparently joined at the hip these days.

"I know, right? Isn't high school the best?" Maggie exclaims.

"You know it!" Annie agrees.

"So what's new?" I ask.

"Can we order first and wait for Ellie to get here; I want everybody to hear," Maggie declares. She hasn't changed a bit.

"There's Ellie." Erin spots her and waves her over our table.

We order two large cheese pizzas before Maggie starts talking.

"Annie and I practically have the same schedule."

Annie chimes in saying, "It's true."

I add, "I was elected class vice president."

"Wow, Eve!" Erin comments, "Congratulations!"

"Thanks. How is your semester going?"

"Great. I've been accepted to do some educational field work in a school in Haiti for part of winter session. I'm excited."

"You're quiet Ellie, I say, what's new with you?"

"Um....well, I'm dating someone..." she bashfully stutters.

"Shut up!" exclaims Maggie. "Spill it."

"His name is Justin; he lives in my building and is really nice. He's from northern Virginia actually."

"Well good for you!" Annie states.

I can't tell if Annie is genuinely excited for Ellie or if she's embarrassed that Ellie found a boyfriend before she did. Because of her reaction, I decide not to mention Matt; it's my first real relationship so who knows what will happen anyway.

"It sounds like everyone is adjusting nicely," Erin says.

"I'm telling you! High school is the best!" Maggie shouts, "I'm afraid it's going to be over before we know it."

"Let's decide right now that we do this again the next time we are here, winter break?"

"Annie, I'll be in Haiti remember?" She says it in an annoying tone almost like she feels Annie never listens to her when she speaks.

"I may be doing winter session at school," Ellie says.

Yep, it's happening, our lives are moving at very different paces and too many different directions. Maggie is right about something too; the three years of high school are going to be over way too soon.

ALTERNATE WORLD

Gina gathers the members of the alternate world in the ballroom and stands behind the podium. She raises her right hand once while she welcomes everyone, and the crowd goes silent.

"As you hopefully already know, you all are very special people, chosen for a very special reason. You have chosen to live your life according to your passion and purpose, not how society says to live your life. You have even managed to stay true to yourself despite pressure from peers or family. It is admirable. That's why you are here in the alternate world."

A resounding clapping from the group slowly emerges before Gina continues.

"We welcome new members into the alternate world on a regular basis. There is always someone choosing themselves for the better. As you can tell, people are inducted into the alternate world in many stages of their lives. Today, however, I'm focused on teenagers. This vulnerable group of individuals continue to be faced with life-altering decisions every single day. If a fifteen or sixteen-year-old can follow the voice in their own heart, they can overcome any obstacle in life. Those are the people we want to invite to the alternate world. Keep your eyes open but don't reveal your status. Remember, the alternate world is only known for those who are lucky enough to join. Keep excelling in your craft. I'm honored to know you all."

The applause erupts again before Gina blows a kiss and steps down from her box before she exits the room.

My World: Chapter Six

Back at school, each month goes by faster than the previous one. Jennifer and Eric are still together after at least three break-ups, each one usually lasting a total of four days. Matt officially leaves in May to spend his third year overseas. We text and meet up occasionally for coffee, but we're not officially together. We mutually decided it will be best for him to focus on his future, plus I want to be able to meet and date more people to enjoy the true boarding school experience.

I am walking back to the dorm to meet up with Jennifer so that we can take our schedules to the bookstore and get our materials straight for next semester.

"Jennifer?" I holler as I unlock the front door. "Jen, are you ready?"

No response. She's not on the couch or in the kitchen. I walk back to her bedroom and find Jennifer hugging the toilet in our adjoining bathroom; she is completely pale.

"Are you okay?"

"Ugh! I don't know what's wrong with me. I have had this flu thing a few months now, off and on; it's awful."

"Jennifer, it's not flu season. You didn't go to the doctor?"

"I thought it was like a twenty-four-hour thing."

"Well, clearly your twenty-four-hour thing has now turned into like a five-week thing. I'm taking you to the clinic."

Before she can object, I grab a vomit bag and escort Jennifer to the shuttle stop. Thankfully, it arrives in moments and takes us to the student clinic a few miles away. I sit in the waiting room while Jennifer is immediately taken to an examination room by a nurse. Twenty minutes pass before Jennifer emerges with a disturbing expression on her face.

"What they'd say?" I nervously ask standing to meeting her.

"They're going to send away my blood work."

"Okay..."

"And they made me pee on a stick." She speaks robotically looking down at the ground. And without looking up adds, "I'm pregnant."

This is truly one of those life moments when no matter what you say, it won't make a difference. It won't make the situation any better. Instead, I give Jennifer a big hug and say, "Everything is going to be okay. Let's get you home."

Needless to say, we don't go to the bookstore. In fact, Jennifer never did get there. She stays in bed every day; her blood work indicates that she is almost two months pregnant, so she is starting to show a tiny bit. When she finally called Eric to tell him, he said it wasn't his and broke up with her. (Turns out that Eric slept with more than one partner throughout their "special relationship", but Jennifer certainly did not.) I walk in our place after class a few days later and find Jennifer sitting up straight and tall on the sofa in the living room.

"I dropped out this morning." Those are the first words out of my roommate's mouth.

"What?" I join her on the couch to get the details.

"I'm moving back home and having this baby."

"Wow! Is that really what you want to do?"

"Believe me, everyone has been trying to talk me out of it, including Eric when he finally acknowledged his role in this situation. My mom has screamed a thousand times about how she never should have sent me to a party school at sixteen. She has also reminded me of all the options available to me." Jennier is now sobbing uncontrollably. "I never in a million years thought this would happen to me, but now it has. This is what I have to do and know this is the right decision for me."

"I don't know what to say." I feel my eyes welling up. "I'm going to miss you so much. You know I will do anything to help you. In fact, I can come visit you every weekend if you'd like."

"Thanks Eve, but I don't want you altering your life. This is my problem. You are on a path to greatness."

"So are you, Jennifer, and you will be an amazing mom. I know it."

We can't stop crying as we embrace; it's been just the two of us from day one. Now, I'll be all by myself (no Jennifer, no Matt, just me). She gets up from the couch with red eyes and flushed cheeks before she says her mom is waiting downstairs to fly home immediately. She packed her two suitcases and told me that she doesn't need any of our shared food or toiletries. We agree to call each other on a daily basis. Then she walks out of our door for her brand-new life, and I realize it's a whole new future for the both of us. When I'm not in class or planning social events for my fellow tenth graders, I am either on the phone with Jennifer or working my tail off in my studies.

Chapter Seven

I have finally gotten used to having a quiet room to myself. My parents came up to visit for a long weekend. We went shopping, sight-seeing, and dining. Unlike at home, there are mounds of snow all around town from Halloween on, and school never closes. So, *what's the point of the snow?*

Jennifer emails me now about three times a week and has learned she will be the proud mother of a baby girl. Her mom plans to help her take care of the infant while Jennifer takes online classes as a partnership between the local high school and community college.

Matt has started texting, calling, and liking all of my pictures on Instagram again. He has suggested that we try and rekindle our relationship. I'm unsure. However, after he and I went out one Friday night, we basically picked up right where we left off. We are walking around the quad one night after dinner holding hands when an 804 number comes through on my cell phone.

"Hello?" I don't recognize the number, but I know it's

somebody from home.

"Eve? It's Maggie! Guess what?" I'm pretty sure I know why she is calling but I allow her to tell me anyway.

"I'm making my debut."

"Congratulations Maggie. I'm excited for you."

"Thanks Eve. You know I want you to be there. Can you make it?"

"Sure Maggie, anything you'd like."

"Great. I'll be in touch! I haven't chosen the date yet, but I know it will be soon. Love ya, bye!"

"Who was that?" Matt asks with great curiosity once I end the call.

"That was Maggie. She went to junior high with me back home."

"And what did she have to say?"

"She's planning her debut."

"Her what?"

"You know when you make your appearance in society."

"I've never heard of such a thing."

"Really?"

"No. It must be a southern thing."

"Maybe." I don't have much to add. My brain is running a thousand thoughts a second about who may be there for this event. I haven't seen anyone from our class since graduation, and I have a feeling a lot of them will be making an appearance at Maggie's event. All I want to do is crawl into bed and call Erin. She'll know what to say. Matt clearly doesn't have a clue.

Erin turns out to be the perfect person to call since she informs me that she will serving as either the program or guest book attendant for the event. What is this, a wedding? I think to myself. Erin changes the subject and proceeds to share some gossip about Ellie too. Evidently, Ellie called Erin bawling about how she loves Justin but is having a hard time coming to agreement on a variety of things. Apparently, Justin likes to be in charge.

"I feel really bad for her, Eve. She's the nicest person on the planet, and I don't want her to get used."

"Relationships are weird, and she's living away from home, so it's probably a lot more going on than just issues with Justin. Hopefully we can check in on her at Maggie's thing. Do you think she'll come home for that?"

"She said she would."

"Cool. Keep me posted. See you soon."

"Talk soon, girl. Bye."

"Bye."

I decide to call Jennifer. Despite everything going on in her life, like a true friend, she asks about our place, if I have a new roommate, my classes, and the situation with Matt these days. We chat for a full forty-five minutes before we simultaneously say *miss and love you*. I'll be excited to be at home for the holiday season.

Despite his attempt to keep me in school for part

of winter break, I let Matt know that I'm going home for the full four weeks to enjoy the festivities and family time. I assure him that I will make it up to him when I return. He has certainly matured all of sudden because all he says he completely understands. I'm going with it. He even takes me to the airport Friday night to catch my flight home. We pull up in front of the terminal, and Matt gets out of the driver's seat to assist me with my luggage. (*Who is this guy?* I wonder.) He gives me a quick kiss on the lips and we say bye. I don't have to wait very long before my plane boards, which is a relief because I'm ready for this break. When I land, I already have a missed call from Maggie and a text message from Annie reminding me what to wear and what time to be at her country club for brunch. Someone is taking their debut very seriously.

Dad is in his usual spot waiting for me after the two-hour direct flight home. This time, because it's so late, I just want to take a shower and get to bed. There will be plenty of time to catch up with everybody. By the time I wake up the following morning, I realize the holidays always go by so much faster than we think they will. Today, I'm supposed to go Christmas tree shopping with Mom and Dad then meet the girls for an afternoon movie. Hope is actually coming home this break with her boyfriend, which means Mom will be cooking some of our childhood favorites for dinner. Note to self: I need to remind myself to enjoy some down time to watch Hallmark Christmas movies while sipping on peppermint hot chocolate.

Hope arrives a few days later with Sam on her arm; he's graduating from college this spring and is obsessed with my big sister. He follows her around the house everywhere she goes. I'm grateful for Dad asking Sam for his help stringing the lights around the porch, so I can finally get some time with Hope by myself. She falls into the wingback chair in the den where I am sprawled out on the couch.

"Hey, Eve. What are you watching?"

"Christmas movie."

"Have you seen this one?"

"I've seen all of them."

"So, how's school going? You're so grown now, already away at school."

"You really think so?"

"I know so. You're 15 almost 16 and practically on your own. I wasn't ready to be on my own at school until I was 18, and honestly, even then I was still unsure."

"Wow, Hope, I never thought about that. Thanks. By the way, in case you didn't know, Sam is obsessed with you."

"You think?"

"This, I know."

"Do you like him?"

"I like him if you like him."

"Thanks Eve. I do. I really like him."

"Then so do I."

She heads over to the couch and gives me a big side hug. "Slide over, Eve, and give me some of those M&M's." We watch the rest of the Christmas movie savoring the chocolate while commentating during every scene. Hope, Mom, and I spend some days running last minute errands for presents. Then, it's neighborhood gatherings, Christmas Mass, and lots of family dinners. Over the weeks, I get more than a few texts from Matt checking in. He tells me he has a present waiting for me when I get back to school. I'll actually be back there in a matter of days. I have to give and receive my own presents, and come Christmas morning, my Santa pile does not disappoint. After we open family gifts and have breakfast, Hope and Sam pack up to spend a few days with Sam's family before they return to school. My sister looks happy. *Isn't that what we are all looking for?* I get to be the only child for a few more days myself, which means I get to pick where I want to go to dinner each night and get doted on. The longer I'm back home, the more I miss it. I'm glad I'm flying home by myself tomorrow so it's an easier transition.

Matt is at Logan International Airport right on time to pick me up and suggests grabbing a bite to eat so that he can hear all about my break. We are seated for just a few moments before he reaches into his backpack and pulls out a little bag.

"This is for you. Merry Christmas."

I'm speechless as I open the bag and pull out a necklace. I can't even speak.

"You don't like it," he says, his expression of disappointment.

"I do. I love it. It just doesn't go with this outfit, but I love it. Thank you."

"I understand."

I put the tiny gift bag in my purse. I truly am appreciative, but I don't think I realize how serious he may be or what he may be expecting. I quickly change the subject to tell him all about my Christmas break and ask him about his. Then I ask if he'd like to return home with me the weekend of March 12th for Maggie's debut day.

"I thought you'd never ask," Matt responds. "I can't wait to meet all of the friends you claim to have."

It's kind of a big deal for me to take a date to a childhood friend's event since everyone will want to know all about Matt so they can secretly judge and then gossip about him (and me) once we have left the premises. I have a few months to prepare for that.

Chapter Eight

Maggie's debut event is breathtaking. She really does look like a princess, which I know she loves. I walk in and give hugs to everyone as soon as I enter the door. Matt finds our place cards and snags our seats at table number five until I join him. When I arrive to the table, I'm delighted to find that Maggie did an exceptional job on the seating arrangements. Except for Annie, who is seated at her family table, all of the girls are assigned to the same table as I am.

"Hi, Lovelies," I greet the ladies.

"You look beautiful," Annie shrieked running over to our table.

"Thank you. So, do you! This is incredible! Who's sitting there?" I pointed to the purse holding a spot.

"That's Erin; she's in the bathroom. And that's Ellie and her boyfriend Justin sitting beside her."

"Awesome. I like our table. Oh Annie, this is Matt."

Matt stands up like such a gentleman and extends his hand.

"Nice to meet you. I take it you're a Kerrington Prep student as well?"

"I am, but this is actually my last full year on campus. I'm spending my final year studying abroad."

"That's so cool!" One of Annie's strengths is that she is always so genuinely interested in meeting new people.

"Eve, is that you?" Erin comes up from behind me with a big hug.

"Erin, what's going on with you?"

"It's spring break for me, so I'm doing fabulously."

"How's school going?"

"I still love it! Thanks for asking."

"Where are Ellie and Justin?" I question.

"I saw them go outside. They haven't come back?" Erin answers.

"I haven't seen them." Sarah chimes in.

"Well, I hope they come in soon; they're about to introduce the debutants."

Just then, Ellie walks in with her boyfriend trailing behind. She whispers hello and quickly takes her seat, no introductions. I know that they have been having issues, but still, he did come with her. The DJ's voice echoed on the microphone as he became our instructor for the rest of the night.

Everyone on your feet. Let's welcome this year's debutant class! Now it's time to enjoy a four-course meal. It's time for the Cupid Shuffle; get on the dance floor. Raise your glass and toast.

I'm so glad I decided to bring Matt and RSVP two for the event. He and I are really going strong as a couple. He made a wonderful impression on all of my friends and family at the event. Since it's our spring break, we have plenty of time to take mini road trips to Boston to enjoy the city life. Since Matt is leaving soon, he's all about taking advantage of the destinations closer to home. At least we have the summer together because I know everything will be different in the fall. All of these thoughts are going through my mind while I'm perusing my many social media accounts. My email dings, indicating that I have something new. It's a *Save the Date* for my sister's wedding. What did I miss?

Chapter Nine

Summer is on the horizon, which means Jennifer's baby girl is arriving soon. I have to decide if I'm going home for the entire summer break or if I'm staying here for a June internship. I kind of want to stay here and take advantage of the time with Matt before we become a long-distance couple. He texts me early in the morning.

We have dinner reservations at 7:30 tonight.

I spend my day on the computer and watching TV until about 6PM when I finally start getting ready. Matt shows up looking incredible in his navy suit and tie. I'm so glad I chose my purple capped sleeved dress and four-inch heels. We take an Uber to the restaurant, check in at the reservation desk, and are seated at a cozy table in the corner.

"Matt, why haven't we ever been to this place before?" I inquire looking all around the swanky restaurant.

"Well, this is a special occasion," Matt says as I beam

with pride.

"That's true. I can't believe you're studying in London next year."

"Oh Eve, you're so cute, but this night isn't just about me. It's about us."

"What do you mean, us?"

"I want tonight to be very special for us."

"Special how?"

"We been together now for months, and you know I would do anything for you. To celebrate our next steps together, I thought we'd stay the night together in the hotel here. My dad booked it for us."

"Stay the night?"

"Yea and get even closer then usual, if you know what I mean."

"I know exactly what you mean, Matt, but-"

Matt cuts me off. "And I love you, Eve! What do you say?"

"I don't think I can, Matt."

"What?" He looks devastated.

"I'm sorry. I love you too, but I can't sleep with you."

"This was a surprise, I know. Maybe you just need some time."

"I don't think time will change my mind. My answer is no. I'm sorry. I'm not ready. I don't know when I'll be ready."

I quickly kiss him on the cheek and stand up to leave.

"Sit down Eve. We're already here and haven't eaten. Let's at least enjoy the meal together."

"Are you sure?"

"I'm sure. I'm just not ready to let you go."

We end up spending the night together in the hotel room his father reserved but in separate beds. This is it for us. I know it. He's moving on. I don't know if I'm making the best decision, but I know I'm making the right one for me, even if it doesn't feel like it right now. The next morning, he and I grab coffee and bagels together before we drive back to town, and he drops me off at school for the last time. Maybe I will go home for all of summer break after all. I find myself pacing around my place rearranging pictures and organizing drawers. In just twenty-four hours, my life is completely different. I know this is called growing up, but I really have no idea how to do it.

I toss and turn all night but can't bear to get out of bed before the sun. I stagger into the kitchen pouring a cup of hot tea when I hear a knock on my door. *Who can that be? Not a lot of people are even on campus this weekend.* I open the door and find a thin, older woman with dirty-blonde hair sitting on top of her head in a neat bun. I notice she is wearing an ornate pink dress. *Do I know her?*

"Hi, Eve." The stranger confidently approaches me.

"Hi?" I reply hesitantly, wondering what she wants.

"I'm Gina."

"Do I know you?"

"No, but I know you, and I've come here to show you something."

"I don't mean to be rude, Gina, but this really isn't a good time."

"I know, and I'm sorry about your break-up with Matt."

I'm taken aback. "How do you know that?"

"Just come with me Eve, I'll drive."

I may not be in a sound mind today as I hesitantly follow Gina to her BMW and jump in the passenger seat. I have no idea where we are going, and I really can't place Gina at all.

ALTERNATE WORLD

We drive about twenty minutes in silence before we arrive at an extremely large house, it's a mansion. I can't for the life of me figure out where we are, and I know I'd remember this giant home with its bright pink door if I had seen it before. Still in awe, I open the car door and follow Gina up the driveway and on to the porch steps. She unlocks the door and I follow her down a narrow white hall. The long hall seems to lead to nowhere until she walks into a grand ballroom full of people. I follow.

"Where are we?" I whisper to her.

"Oh my gosh! Eve Thompson!" A short woman with dark brown hair comes bouncing toward us. "I should have known you'd be one of us. Welcome."

"Thank you, I think. Where are we? And do I know you?"

Gina jumps in and the woman sheepishly disappears, "She knows you because you are a world-renowned attorney representing high profile women."

"No, I'm not. I am a student at Kerrington Prep. I'm going to be a second year in the fall."

"That is true in one world, but here in alternate world, you have already achieved your purpose. This is who you will be in the real world and who you are working toward becoming today. And in your case, you've been very well known here for years. You have appeared in just about every major magazine and newspaper.

"Wait a minute. My purpose?" I ask.

"Yes, your purpose in the alternate world."

"Alternate world?" I stutter.

"Yes, this is the alternate world, and you are now here."

"Where are we? Who else is here?"

"You'll see."

Gina is extremely vague. How come I've never heard of this place before? I start thinking I finally must have fallen asleep and this is all a dream, but the nudge on my arm is quite real when Gina moves me forward. We walk down yet another hallway where she points out portraits on the wall. I recognize images of some civil rights leaders and some First Ladies. I'm admiring all of the famous photographs and stop suddenly in front of a huge black and white image of a beautiful woman with hazel eyes.

"Wait a minute, wait, wait...I've seen this picture before. Is that my great, great grandmother?"

"Yes, it is. She was a lovely lady," Gina smiles, eyeing the snapshot as she speaks.

"You knew her?"

"Of course I did."

"How on earth could you have known her? How old are you?"

"Now Eve, you know that's not the type of question you ask a woman."

Embarrassed, I look down and say, "I'm sorry, but none of this makes any sense to me."

Gina laughs in a high pitch voice like a fairy before she speaks again.

"As the keeper of the alternate world, Eve, I have no age. I've greeted every single individual showcased in this hallway."

"I don't understand." I am confused, irritated, and still wondering what is happening to me."

"It's hard to comprehend at first. I can see you are perplexed. Let's get something to eat."

"I feel eating is the last thing I need to do right now. Can you tell me how you know my great, great grandmother and all of these famous people and why I am here?"

"Let's sit."

All of a sudden, a pink sofa appears in the narrow hallway positioned neatly against the wall. I reluctantly sit and angle my legs toward Gina. I study her expression and listen intently so I can decipher exactly what she is saying to me.

"Like I said before, this is the alternate world. Not everyone belongs here. Your great, great grandmother did, these powerful leaders from our nation's history did, and you do."

"How is this possible?" Nothing is registering for me.

"You, like all of these people before you have followed your heart's desires and made a choice that is right for you."

"What do you mean?"

"You really have no idea?"

"Not a clue!"

"You're a fifteen-year-old girl in boarding school away from home surrounded by boys, girls, peer pressure, partying, and everything a teenager experiences in their lifetime. Are you with me so far?"

"I guess so..."

"I understand Matt asked you to have sex with him last night, correct?"

"Uh-huh."

"And you said no. Do you know how hard that is to do?"

"I haven't really thought about it like that."

"Eve, saying no to the norm and being true to you is the hardest thing in the world to do, especially for young women. Your friends are now in relationships, and everyone is growing up in their own way. You could have gone along with it and given in like so many girls do. You could have finally said you "did it", but you didn't. Despite the route that your peers and strangers are taking in life, you stood up for yourself and chose what makes you happy. That takes courage. Because of your actions last night, you are initiated into the alternate world today."

"But what if I don't want to be? No offense, but I've managed to survive on my own for a little while now."

"Yes, you have, but you also haven't had to face such tough decisions in your time before. Your teenage years are the hardest. We want you to maintain your path of greatness to achieve your ultimate purpose. We don't want you to fall by the wayside."

"What about my life?"

"This is part of your life. You now have two lives." Gina reaches over to hold my hand. It's only been a few hours, Eve. I know you are feeling overwhelmed, but there is still a lot more information to obtain whenever you are ready."

"You hungry?" Gina asks while a magnificent spread is immediately placed in front of us by two men dressed in tuxedos. "Eat up."

"Who are those people?"

"Oh, they work here, whatever you need."

"They work in this mansion?"

"They work in this world; it continues far beyond these four walls. This is just our central meeting place."

I guess that makes sense. I am trying hard to convince myself that this is just a regular adventure, a tale to tell later on.

"You know, Eve, you remind me a lot of your great,

great grandmother, Edith," Gina pauses.

"Really? I can't believe you actually knew her. I've only heard stories. She was my father's great grandmother. What was she like?"

"Oh, she was incredible; quite the lady. Everyone looked up to her. She was one of the big female leaders of the women's suffrage movement in the late 1880's. She spoke at churches and women's groups around the nation sharing the importance of gender equality and women's rights."

"Oh my gosh...my great, great grandmother?"

"Yes. She was way ahead of the times. In my personal opinion, she should have made the history books."

"Wow!" I can't believe this iconic figure is related to me.

"In fact, when she was working hard to move females forward, traditional women spoke out against her suggesting she was improper and a threat to all of them. Nevertheless, Edith knew what was right for the future generations, including yours, and despite controversy, continued moving forward. That was the moment when she was invited to her alternate world. In her life, she married, raised a family, your family, and wrote articles about her work. Here, in our world, she was also a proclaimed political leader, which was her life-long purpose, and just forty-six-years-old when women finally earned the right to vote."

"How come my family never knew any of this?"

"Nobody knows about the alternate world except those who are in it. You can't talk about it in your regular life. It's the unknown."

"Tell me about it!" I respond.

"You are very fortunate to have a family member here to watch over you," Gina proclaimed," Not very many people do."

"Do people die in the alternate world?"

"Yes. Your death date in life is the same as your death date here. No one lives forever. Imagine the crowds! Anyway, to answer your question, when you die, we commemorate your true identity and purpose by adding the portrait to our hallway. When your great grandmother died of pneumonia, she died here as well. The difference is no matter how much time passes, our spirits always surround us with the same strength. The spirits that have lived in the alternate world are still heavily felt here and can be felt from people like you in the real world. In spirit years, there is no difference between a year ago or a hundred years ago. Your great-great grandmother's spirit is still here. There is quite a bit of greatness in this world. You will feel it at every moment from here on out. It stays with you in your "normal" life too; you won't be able to escape it."

"When do I go back to my normal life?"

"Whenever you wish. You can go back and forth between the two worlds as you please. Of course, I'll have to drive you home today to be sure you arrive back safely to your daily life. After today, you can do whatever you please, but we hope to see you often, Eve. You are a very special individual. We are so happy to have you as one of us."

"Thanks, Gina. I really appreciate that. I think I just need some time to process it all."

"I completely understand. This is not my first rodeo," she laughs. Whenever you have any questions, you know where to find me. I'll introduce you to some more people next time to help you feel more comfortable with your journey. How does that sound?"

"Sounds good."

"Great. Are you ready to go?"

"I'm ready. I had a whole day planned."

"Oh, don't worry, Eve, your day didn't go to waste. That's something you will get used to. You're in another world, not another time zone. When I drop you back home, it will be the same exact time as it was when I knocked on your door this morning."

"Oh, wow, I really don't know how I'm going to get used to it."

"Pretty soon, your alternate world will be second nature."

Gina drives me back home (again about 20 minutes with not a single bit of traffic-so weird). I open the door to the apartment and my coffee mug is sitting on the counter with steam still rising from it. The clock on the microwave says 9:03am. *This is the weirdest day.* I cannot wrap my mind around what has happened already this morning, and I apparently have a full day ahead of me. *Get it together, Eve!* I run errands and meet up with some classmates for lunch. At 2PM, I feel like it's 11:00 at night, so I lie on my bed and stare at the ceiling; a thousand thoughts run through my mind.

How did Gina find me? Who is she exactly? How am I a famous lawyer all of a sudden? Do I know anyone else in the alternate world? How do I balance living in two different lives?

I need to get some answers. I won't get any sleep tonight, so I jump in my car and drive to the mansion. I'm hoping to recall some landmarks from the drive this afternoon. Obviously, I do because I pull right up in front of the house without issue. *So weird.* Gina is standing on the porch waiting for me.

"I knew you'd be back, Eve! Come on in. I'm ready to answer any questions you may have."

"It could take a while," I yell back at her as I walk up the stairs.

"I have all the time in the world." She chuckles and opens the front door.

"That's my first question actually. How do you live forever and never age?"

"I have never lived in the real world. I was placed here

solely to lead the alternate world and recognize people who do extraordinary things or choose a different path from the pack. I'm constantly seeking individuals who are living out their purpose and who define themselves by their convictions. Unfortunately, I don't find people every day, but you were brought to my attention last night. Well, you know the story."

"Do I know anyone else here that I can talk to about this?"

"You do actually. I don't know if they're here right now or not. Let's go see."

Down the hall past the paintings; I swear I notice Great, Great Grandmother Edith wink at me. This time, we enter a giant ballroom with people standing all around and socializing; it looks like a party. Gina and I stand in the doorway observing everybody. A girl walks in beside us and beelines over to the bar (the men in tuxedos are serving drinks).

"I know her," I point and say.

"You do?" Gina doesn't seem to believe me.

'Well, I don't really know her, but I've definitely seen her before."

"Yes, you probably have. That's Melinda; she attended Kerrington Prep for a semester.

"That's right! She was always at Matt's house parties."

"She wasn't always there."

"What do you mean?"

"She was there in the fall until she had an incident with one of Matt's teammates."

"Do you know which one?"

"I only really know the people who are tapped to be in the alternate world. In this case, that would be Melinda, but I believe I've heard the name Eric before."

"Eric? Are you sure?"

"I'm 99.9% sure! These stories are my life, you know."

"Oh my gosh! I have to tell Jennifer."

"Eve, darling, you cannot talk to anyone about this."

This is going to be harder than I thought. I didn't realize my worlds would collide so closely.

"Well, will you tell me the story?"

"From what I understand, it's a case of how social media has the power to be as hurtful as it does to be helpful. Melinda is very quiet, shy, and very trusting. Like you, she wanted to be social and friendly, but some men felt she wasn't giving her attention where attention was due. Eric created a fake handle to spread some pretty nasty rumors about Melinda on social media platforms. It was shared with a number of young men around the campus."

"Oh, my gosh! How did I not know this?"

"Clearly, you were not on the receiving end of this cruelty. These guys criticized her looks, her character, and made up lies about her behavior. It was horrible. Melinda never sunk to their level and never gave in even though she was completely ridiculed online. Her reputation was ruined. She held her head high, maintained her composure, and stayed on campus to complete her semester. I met her in her dorm room the last day she was enrolled in the school."

"Wow! I had no idea!"

"She has since transferred to an all-girls' school in the south."

"I feel so bad."

"You didn't know, but now you do, so you can be a friend to her. She is just another example of greatness that we honor here in the alternate world. She's a therapist, specializing in counseling of teenagers considering suicide. She certainly considered it for her own life but managed to find her strength inside herself, with the support of friends and family. Not everyone is that fortunate, so Melinda is that difference."

"How is she here right now when her school is down south?"

"This is an alternate world Eve, not an alternate city. Everyone can get here just like you. Whenever you need to come here, you can be here in a matter of minutes."

"Sorry. It's still so foreign to me."

"It's okay. Would you like to talk to her?"

"I don't know if she will remember me."

"Trust me. This is a safe space. We all know that what it takes to be here is never easy. She will be glad to see a familiar face. Go ahead. You got this."

I walk over to the snack bar where she is standing and introduce myself.

"Excuse me, you look so familiar, did you go to Kerrington Prep?

"I did. I'm Melinda."

"Hi, Melinda. I'm Eve."

"Eve Thompson? Weren't you our class president?"

"Guilty as charged."

"I can see you being a lawyer in the future."

"That's what I'm hearing. How'd you guess?"

Melinda gives me a look that tells me she already knew I was brought into the alternate world and knows what my purpose is here.

"Melinda, how long have you been here?" I ask.

"Wow, I don't even know, I guess about seven months."

"This is my first day."

"Weird, isn't it?"

"I'm so glad to hear you say that."

"I completely understand. I was very taken off guard when Gina first met me. I don't know if you know my situation."

I nodded while she continued.

"I couldn't confide in my roommate or family but had to trust this stranger in pink. I was having major trust issues. It made no sense at all to follow this woman, but at the time it just felt right."

"Yea, I know what I mean," I added.

"This world we were born into is full of people who have made tough decisions and who live with it every single day, often being judged for it in the process. In the alternate world, there is only acceptance and support of each other. It's an incredible feeling. Sometimes, you will find that you will want to spend more of your life here than in the regular world, especially when you need a reminder that you made the right choice."

"So, you go back and forth on a regular basis?"

"That I do, but you have to do what works for you. Just remember, you were true to yourself, and you followed your heart's desires. That's why you're here. Welcome to the family, Eve. Call me anytime. Gina will tell you how to get in touch." She gives me a hug and walks away. Gina comes over to check on me.

"How was that exchange?"

"It was fine. I'm beginning to see why this world is so sacred. It saves a lot of people."

"I guess it does in a way. Nobody really talks about why they are here. Only you and I know, but you should know that everyone here has only good intentions. You can feel at home here. You can be yourself."

"It's getting late. Guess I should be heading back."

"Remember, Eve, there is no time lost here."

"Oh yea."

"Also, I want you to know that you shouldn't use this world as an escape. You must live your life to the fullest. Make decisions that make you happy. Create relationships and live out your largest dreams. Know that we will support you in every decision that you make. See you soon!"

"See you soon, Gina." Thanks again. I'll try my best to get the hang of it."

"I know you will, dear. Until next time…"

And she is gone. I return to my place and again, it's the same time as when I left.

My World: Chapter Ten

Gina is right. I have to focus on my actual life not this dream life. I somehow need to create a balance between my real world and my alternate world. It's just going to have to be something to get used to; if my great, great grandmother was able to do it, so can I. Erin is coming to visit tomorrow for Memorial Day weekend. She is going to Haiti for a summer mission trip, and I'm staying around here for much as the summer as originally planned, but not with Matt. I applied and was accepted to be a junior camp counselor position in Boston. They have a great connection with my school, so they hire rising second-year students; they also provide cabin housing for every counselor. It's a win-win. High school kids around the country apply for the opportunity, so it's a great addition to my future college application. Exhausted, I prepare frozen food for dinner, my version of a home cooked meal, and go to bed early. It's going to be another busy day.

I wake up, shower, and get dressed for a day of shopping. I need more summer clothes. I know Erin will want to explore the downtown today. Erin texts me on Friday afternoon at 4PM Pacific time when she arrives at the airport; I am waiting in the arrival area looking for Erin at the Jet Blue terminal. She walks out the automated doors with sunglasses on and a huge smile. She's waving at me like I don't see her.

"EVE!!! How are you?!?" I hop out of the car and give her a quick hug before placing her suitcase on the shuttle.

"Hi, Erin. I'm so glad to see you. Are you starving?"

"I could eat."

"Cool. The shuttle will drop us off at school, so we can drop your stuff off at my place then we can walk to get a bite out for dinner. I can't wait to hear what's going on with you. Sound good?"

"Sounds great!"

We choose a corner restaurant downtown with a great crowd for us to eat, talk, and talk some more.

"Eve, do you just love it up here? What's new?"

"I do love it; this is my home now for sure. I'm starting a new job in about a week. Orientation day is Monday. How's the school year going? When does summer vacation start for you all?"

"It's going well. We have exams next week then one more week, then I go to Haiti."

"Yes. Are you excited?"

"Very excited. So how's Matt?"

"Don't be mad. I haven't really told anyone."

"What?"

"We broke up."

"I'm sorry."

"Don't be. He's studying abroad next year, and he's a whole three years ahead of me. It wouldn't work out anyway." *I know she's my best friend, but I don't want to go into the details.*

"You're kidding?"

"No, it just didn't feel right."

"Well, good for you."

"Thanks."

"This looks like a good spot to meet someone new."

I look around and notice a large group of boys around our age at the high-top tables.

"Why do you think I picked it?" We both laugh then study the menus.

Erin and I did a low-key night of movies until we both pass out. We sleep in, then head to breakfast together before she has to fly out to meet her cousins for their holiday event.

"So, do you hang out a lot with Annie and Maggie?

"I don't see Maggie as much outside of school these days."

"Oh really? I didn't know that."

"I don't think a lot of people know. I kind of feel like after her debut, she shifted friendship circles. She hangs out with Annie still but a lot of girls that go to the country club with her."

"I can see that."

"I know, right. Pretty predictable."

"I hardly ever hear from them. You need to plan your next trip to come back on a weekend during the school year."

"You can count on it. Should we go?"

"Yes, you never know about security on a Saturday."

We pay the tab then hop on the shuttle to the airport. We pull up in front of the Jet Blue doors and say goodbye. I hop back on the shuttle and head straight back home to prepare for my first day as camp counselor tomorrow.

I toss and turn all night long. It's the feeling of the unknown. I'm also worried that I will oversleep and miss the bus into the city for orientation. I hop out of bed at 6:15 and get dressed, selecting a black and white striped sundress for my first day. After looking in the mirror at least five times, I decide it's finally time to go to my initial meeting. Hopefully, the bus is on time.

After a 45-minute ride, I arrive at the stop two blocks away from the camp. I'm greeted on the front steps by one of the camp counselors, a girl who looked about a year or so older than me.

"Good morning, Miss Eve. Welcome to Camp Wonder. Allow me to lead you to our dining hall for the welcome breakfast."

I follow her into a large room with circular tables and wheelchairs. An assortment of bagels, fruit, and pastries fill the center of the table. Mr. Parker, the head of the camp, greets me as I enter the room.

"Eve, welcome to Camp Wonder. We are so glad to have you join our team. Come on in and we'll get settled." He stands at the head of the table. "Everybody, this is Eve Thompson."

Everyone, who is already seated and eating breakfast, waves and says hello. Another young girl, tall, slender with jet-black straight long hair, at the table stands and motions to me to come down to the open seat beside her.

I thank her and make my own plate before orientation begins. *Is this a daily thing?* I wonder (no pun intended). Following the meeting, the same girl, Violet, tells me that I will be working with her today to set up the ballroom for the campers' welcome event. I follow her to meet a team of people blowing up balloons, hanging streamers, and welcome packets. We reconvene for lunch with the other camp counselors, twenty of us in total, and listen to Mr. Parker give us the expectations, daily duties, and list of campers starting in two days.

At the end of the initial workday, I take the bus back and get off at a stop that I swear is close to the mansion. I haven't been in over a week, and I'm specifically drawn to it this evening.

ALTERNATE WORLD

I begin walking down the city sidewalk then turn on a dusty path. In the clearing, I see the outline of the mansion, so I start walking faster. Just like before, Gina greets me at the door and asks how my first day of the new job went.

"How did you know, Gina?" I am truly surprised.

"I know everything about the members of our alternate world," Gina replies very matter of fact.

Note to self. Gina knows everything.

"Come on in, dear, and have some dinner. You must be hungry between the bus ride and walk. There's someone here tonight that I believe you know."

I follow Gina into the dining room where a man in a tuxedo is standing at the end of table waiting to take my order. I have a hankering for a cheeseburger and French fries; in this world, my wish is their command. I tell Gina the details about my new job and the fact that I'm going to be very busy all summer but am super excited. She starts to tell me about the social at the mansion happening in two weeks that everyone is invited to attend. While she's speaking, I look past her closely watching a tall brunette. She doesn't look exactly how I remember, but I know it's her.

"Jennifer?!" I hop off the stool to run after her until she finally turns around.

"Eve? Is that you? Oh my gosh! It's so great to see you. What are you doing here?"

Gina has now joined the two of us pretending as though she is surprised we have gravitated toward each other.

"Eve entered our world about a week ago. How do you two know each other?"

Jennifer excitedly says, "We were roommates at school."

"Well, then, you two have a lot of catching up to do." Gina continues, "I'll leave you to talk."

Eve says, "Have you eaten? I'm waiting on a burger over there."

"I'll join you!"

"This is so crazy, Jennifer, you have to tell me what's happening. How long have you been here?"

"I know! I'm so glad to see someone here from my old life. You know we can't talk to anybody about this?"

"I know! Another girl from our school is here too."

"You mean Melinda? I know. She dated one of Eric's best friends."

"Really?" My tone suggests that I know something that she doesn't know.

"Yes, obviously he and Eric are cut from the same mold. Melinda was clearly the smart one."

"You have no idea!" And then I quickly want to change the subject.

"How is your daughter?"

"She's wonderful- the only thing Eric ever did that was good."

No such luck, let me try another question.

"How is it being back home?"

"It's good. I go to a high school where they let you bring your children to go in the day care center. I take classes there at the community college at night and I have been volunteering (when I can) at the hospital."

"Wow, Jennifer! You're doing so much. I'm just trying to balance school classes during the semester and a summer job that starts in two days."

"Believe me, you're doing it right. I couldn't imagine a life without my baby girl, but I believe this is the path I'm supposed to follow. I'm making it work."

"I'm so lucky to know you, Jennifer. You're the best. Now tell me what happened. How did you get here?"

"I think about that all of the time; I know the basic reason why I'm here, but I always wonder why I was chosen."

"I feel the same way....so tell me."

"I had taken Annabelle, my daughter, to one of those jungle gym places."

"That sounds fun."

"Believe me, you're not missing anything. Moms go to these indoor playgrounds to get out of the house and socialize with other mothers. I'm the youngest one by far."

"I can see that."

"I was sitting on a bench watching Annabelle slide around on the mats when I heard a bang and brief scream from the snack bar area. A little boy was on the ground passed out. I bolted up and ran over to elevate his head and start resuscitation until the paramedics arrived."

"So you saved this little boy's life?"

"The hospital has really taught me a lot. I know that's where I want to work after school."

"This is an incredible story. You're a hero."

"I wouldn't go that that far. More like right place, right time."

"And your life here?"

"Turns out, I'm a world-renowned surgeon."

"That's amazing, Jen. Or should I say Dr. Jen? Congratulations, and you deserve it!"

"It's definitely a dream come true with a few bumps along the way." She and I both break out into laughter. "Now how did you get here?"

"My story is not as admirable as yours."

"Oh stop. Tell me, and by the way, how is Matt?"

"Funny you should ask. Matt and I broke up."

"You did? That must have been hard."

"Surprisingly, it wasn't. He wanted something more. It didn't feel right."

"You have to follow your heart. Intuition is a real thing, you know?"

"That's what Gina said when the very next morning she was standing at my front door."

"You know Gina only visits people who do something difficult or different from most people."

"That's what she told me."

"It's true. It's all about the path you're destined to be on. This is yours."

"And yours." She smiles before she starts again.

"So, have you talked to Matt?"

"Not since that night. I don't think I'm really his favorite person anymore; I never heard from him again."

"You will. They always come back."

"I don't think I want to hear from him. Let's change the subject. How often do you come here?"

"Not as much as I'd like, but when I do everything makes so much sense. I'm more of a big picture person anyway. It's nice here to be able to shut out the noise with no distractions. No cell phone service, no social media, no Snipchit, or whatever they call it."

"Well, I have missed you. How lucky are we to be

reunited?"

"Apparently, we are two of a kind."

Gina approaches our table with an evident bright glow in her eyes but doesn't say a word.

Like little kids, Jen and I both enthusiastically say, "What?!"

Gina just smiles, "I love when old friends from the real world connect here in the alternate world as well. It doesn't happen very often. It just goes to show you that you two are very special women. You were destined to be here."

Jennifer and I exchange a look meaning the same thing. *We still aren't quite clear how out of the millions of people on earth, she and I are two of the chosen ones into this world.* I intend to find out.

"I hate to spoil this lovely reunion young ladies, but it is getting late, and you know you have a whole evening ahead of you."

"She's right Eve. No matter how many hours we spend here, the time hasn't moved back home. I have to pick Annabelle up from my mother's and get dinner on the table. Will I see you again soon?"

"I hope so!" We give each other a big hug knowing we really won't know when it will be. Then, we return to our respective lives.

My World: Chapter Eleven

Once I get home, I see a voicemail has appeared on my phone. I press play before removing and tossing the shoes I have been in all day long onto the kitchen floor.

Hey Eve. It's Erin. Have you talked to Ellie by chance? I'm really worried about her. She and Justin were in town this week, and we were meeting for lunch on the grove. I got to the restaurant first and while I was walking in, I heard shouting. Anyway, I turned around in the doorway; she and Justin were screaming at each other walking down the side-walk (he was about ten steps ahead of her). She texted me a few minutes later saying she wouldn't be able to meet me for lunch. She has no idea I saw her. We have to talk. I'm worried about her. Call me.

Ellie is such a quiet person and keeps everything to her-self. If her relationship was bothering her, she would never reveal it. I will just have to pretend I don't know anything. Maybe she is awake right now. *Is Ohio east-*

ern or central time? I can never remember anything about that state. I dial her cell number anyway and wait for her voicemail.

"Hello?" Ellie answers after five rings.

"Hi Ellie. It's Eve."

"Eve, how are you?"

"I'm great. How are you doing?"

"I'm fine."

"Good. I heard you were back home this week."

"Just for a few days."

"How's Justin?"

"He's okay."

"Well, I want to find a time when we can all hang out again. It's been a while."

"I agree. I will check my calendar and let you know."

"Sounds great!"

"Okay, thanks for calling, Eve. I've gotta run, but I'll call you back soon."

"Alright, take care, Ellie."

"Bye, Eve."

Erin is right; something is going on with Ellie, and she is not going to say a word. I will call and report an update to her in the morning; I have some emails to take care of before the early morning welcome meeting.

I am so excited about my new summer job, but 7:30 meetings are too early for me. For this one, in addition to waking up at dawn and getting ready, I still need to get on the bus in time to make it across town. Tomorrow is the first day of camp for the children. On another note, I still have so many questions left to be answered by Gina. I may head over to the mansion this evening. This time, I will bring a change of clothes.

ALTERNATE WORLD

Evidently, Gina senses my visit since she is standing in the entrance way when I walk in after a long day of work.

"I know you have questions, my dear." She says in the foyer. "You should ask me all of them tonight, everything you want to know, so you can finally feel comfortable with your new life."

"How did you know?"

"All of the newbies go through this in the beginning. Someone out there on earth will be making a life-changing decision soon and will need my guidance and full attention soon enough. This evening, however, is for you. My time is yours."

"That is actually related to my first question. How did you choose me?"

"I know you were happy with Matt and that you were truly hoping for the best, so you choosing your boundaries over him was a very hard thing to do, especially with all of your friends and your sister in serious relationships."

"How did you know about Hope?"

"Do I have you to remind you again that I know everything?" She smiles lovingly.

"I need to remind myself not to doubt you. I'm sorry, Gina."

"Not at all, dear. The important part to me is how you respond to your life change, and you have done so beautifully so far. You are young, and you have your whole life ahead of you. You are on the right course to achieving your goals and dreams."

"When I talked with Jennifer, she implied she was in here for saving a young child."

"I greeted her the day after that action she took, but that isn't the reason she is here."

"Does she know the reason?"

"She knows. You should ask her next time."

I wonder why she didn't tell me in the first place.

"What about her being a world-renowned surgeon?"

"In this world she is, which means everything she's doing in the real world will lead her to this position and title, and that is how she will be remembered."

"Like how my great grandmother was remembered?"

"That is correct."

"And what about me? How I will be remembered?"

"Personally, I don't know quite yet, but professionally, you will be remembered for exactly what you were told when you first arrived. Every meeting, summer camp job, or relationship you are currently developing is a part of the path that will lead you to becoming a famous defense lawyer for high profile women. Now, remember, while there is greater plan for you, you are still responsible for the decisions you make throughout your life."

"I understand. I'm assuming my parents are not part of this world. Am I right? Actually, do you have a directory of members, so I know who is in this world? It really would be helpful."

"Haha, that would kind of defeat the purpose of having a safe place for individuals to live their lives accordingly. And no, your parents are not part of this world at this time."

My parents, the two people who taught me exactly how to be me, are not in this world. How can that be? I guess I'll never know.

"But there's still a possibility that they can join?"

"There's always a possibility. It only takes one single moment or decision to change or define an individual significantly."

"And what about my sister?"

"What about her?"

"How can I ensure that she joins me here?"

"You can't. People have to live their own lives, create their own path, and be true to themselves. Like you, only she can make her own decisions. Time will tell."

"So what about my life now?"

"Because of a brave choice you made, you now have

the luxury of two lives. You will continue to live your life however you choose to. You already know what you are working toward; think of it as a roadmap. In this world, you are already recognized as such and you will always be remembered and admired as one of us.

"I think I get it. I guess that's all then."

I look down at the floor still baffled by the entire situation. *Is this really how it is from now on? Am I really living a part of my life without my entire family?*

"Are you sure?"

"I guess so." I know there's nothing else for me to say.

"Well let me say this. You were chosen for your truth and uniqueness, don't let us down."

"I won't. Thank you, Gina for everything. I am eternally grateful."

"We are delighted to have you dear. Good night, and safe travels home."

My World: Chapter Twelve

I decide to walk home and process everything Gina has shared with me. I need to not worry so much about what my life will look like in the future but instead enjoy each day in the present. There is no guarantee for tomorrow. Gina and Great-Great Grandmother are looking over me. Tomorrow, I will start anew. I also want to call Jennifer and find out exactly what Gina is talking about. I can't imagine Jennifer keeping anything from me, but we certainly weren't as close when she left school and moved back home. I keep walking until my building appears in the clearing, and I am home.

Sure enough, I wake up the following morning with a new-found spirit, eager to learn and grow both personally and professionally. I know it sounds cheesy, but it makes sense to me. I spend extra time straightening my hair before I put on my camp counselor outfit and pack my bag for the three-week adventure. (The families start moving their children in at 10am this morning). I stop in the bagel shop near the camp and order a sesame bagel toasted with butter to go. The cashier hands me my receipt and change and directs me to stand to the left and listen for my number. In the process of putting money back into my wallet, I drop coins. Before I can bend down, someone is standing in front of me holding the quarters.

"I believe these are yours."

I am taken back by the chivalry of the tall, handsome stranger dressed in a coat and tie.

"Thank you." I can't help but stare at his beautiful brown skin and dark eyes.

"You're welcome. Do you come here often? This place is always busy."

"I just started a new job four blocks up, and I needed a convenient breakfast."

"Number 112!" Someone shouts from the kitchen.

"Oh, that's me!" I exclaim.

I return to the man, "What did you order?"

"I already ate. I was just headed out. Can I walk you somewhere?"

"That would be nice."

He opens the door for me to go out ahead of him, and we head in the same direction.

'I'm Eve, by the way."

"Ben."

"Where are you headed, Ben?"

"Three more blocks."

"What's there?"

"I'm doing a summer internship at my dad's law firm."

"Are you serious?"

"Yes, why?"

"That's what I'd love to do one day."

"One day, huh?"

"Yes!"

"Where are you headed today?"

"I'm a camp counselor at Camp Wonder this summer."

"How do you like it?"

"I love it so far, but it's only been two days. The kids move in today."

"That sounds fun."

My road to camp arrives first. I wave good-bye to Ben and thank him for the walk.

"Do you want to meet for bagels again in the morning?" he asks.

"I would love to, but I'm actually having breakfast with ten-year-old girls this week. How about Saturday morning? 9am?

"I will see you then, Eve."

Clearly my new attitude is a good one. I'm still smiling when I walk up the stairs to Camp Wonder. The head counselor hands all of the junior counselors, including me, our cabin assignments, and the list of the four girls in our cabins with us. At 10am, we are directed to stand in front of our cabins to greet the families of the children we will be working with this week. Four eight-year-old girls from up and down the east coast are assigned to me.

During lunch, I decide to text Jennifer to plan a time for us to meet at the mansion. We decide on meeting this weekend after camp session #1 is complete. Until then, my entire week will involve chaperoning meals, arts and crafts, outdoor activities, movie night, campfires, and so much more. This first day flies by, and before I know it, I'm lying in bed staring at the ceiling already fantasizing about Ben.

What is his story? Saturday can't come fast enough.

Even though I'm responsible for the safety of a few little girls this week, I still receive phone calls from my own mom asking me if I'm eating and getting plenty of sleep. I know she wanted me to come home for the entire summer, but I will be there soon enough. I can't lie; it will be wonderful to have someone taking care of me every day. I love being on my own, but according to the law, I'm still a child and even though we don't like to admit it, children need their parents.

After five straight days of roasting marshmallows, singing songs, sailing, and eating three meals a day with elementary school children, it is time to say good-bye to these campers and prepare for the new arrivals. A few children stay for all three weeks, but the majority of kids are locals who come for the five days of fun. Tonight, I have the cabin all to myself, which is a good thing because I need some beauty rest before tomorrow. I learned this week that the giggles of little girls can last far into the night. Peace and quiet is exactly what I need.

I choose a little gray dress with strappy sandals to wear Saturday morning. You have to dress to impress, especially a boy. (They are so visual.) Ben is already sitting at a corner table when I saunter in the door; he waves at me (as if I hadn't noticed his beautiful face).

"Good morning, Eve. What can I get you for breakfast?"

"You don't have to get me anything. I can order."

"I know I don't have to. I want to."

"In that case, I'd love a bagel, toasted with butter and a coffee with one sugar. Thank you."

"No problem, I'll be right back."

I watch him confidently, yet politely, interact with the ladies behind the counter. *Maybe Monday morning's encounter was meant to be.*

"Do you have any appointments today?" I ask Ben when he returns to the table.

"Nothing until this afternoon. I'm helping my dad with a project. What about you?"

"Today is my day off. Camp resumes again on Monday.

"Great, so we have enough time for our first date."

"This is a date?"

"I hope so, and if it goes well, I'd love to plan a dinner

date sometime soon."

I blush and then smile before continuing with the conversation.

"Well then, tell me about yourself." I pause and wait for his response.

"Alright, let's see. I was born and raised outside Boston. Where you are from?"

"I'm from Virginia. I'm up here for school. I go to Kerrington Prep."

"No way. I go to the public high school around the area."

"You do?"

"Yes. My dad's office is here, so I'm around the city a lot too."

"That's good to know. I just started my summer job here last week. Actually, my first day was last Monday when I met you."

"Well, that explains why I had never seen you before that day," Ben says grinning before he blows on his coffee, then takes a quick sip.

"True. So, when you're not working with your dad, what do you do in your spare time?"

"Good question. I like to go running or paddle boarding at the beach. What about you?"

"I would say going to a movie or reading by the pool or beach would be ideal for me."

I see Ben glance at his watch and assume my answer

is not appealing enough for him.

"What time is it?" I ask him.

"Sorry," he responds, "I am a stickler for being on time, but I don't want to rush our conversation."

"I'm down for continuing it another time, if you'd like?"

"Yes, I will go on a date with you."

Caught off guard, I stumble with my words and can't get anything out. I feel my cheeks getting redder by the second as I avoid eye contact.

"I'm just kidding," he interrupts. "That would be great. How about dinner next Friday night? We can drive to a place near the water."

"I'd love that!"

"Cool, go ahead and put your number in my phone so I can give you a call." He watched me do that, then said, Sounds great. Ready to go?"

"Yes."

We take the same path and walking position as last time, him to his dad's office and me back to camp.

"Thanks for breakfast, Ben. Good luck with your appointment."

"It was my pleasure, Eve. See you on Friday, if not beforehand."

"See you then."

I hang out with some of the camp counselors for the afternoon. I know I'm sneaking out tonight to meet

Jennifer at the mansion. The gang and I decide to order take-out for dinner. The buzzer rings outside of the dining hall, and the delivery guy stands holding our Chinese food absolutely drenched.

"It's raining outside?" I ask puzzled.

"Monsooning. Just started," he briefly responds.

I eat my wonton noodles and fried rice before opening my fortune cookie. *A Fresh Start Will Put You On Your Way.* I put it in my pocket to hang up later. I'm dying to see Jennifer and ask her everything tonight; when I look up at the clock it finally says 7:30pm. Thirty minutes until meeting time. I'm glad there's an extra umbrella here. I say goodbye to the crew. It is still pouring when I head outside and walk to the bus stop down the street.

ALTERNATE WORLD

I'm driving toward the mansion and can't believe my eyes when the rain suddenly halts as I approach the front steps. The sun is shining, and as usual it's a perfect 72 degrees. *What is the deal with this place?*

Gina greets me at the door, as usual; her smiling face is always wonderful and so comforting to see.

"Hello, Miss Eve! It's lovely to see you this evening."

"Hi, Gina. Did it rain here today?"

Gina laughs the loudest, heartiest laugh. "No!"

"Does it ever rain here?"

"Well, of course not, Eve."

"How is that possible? It has been pouring all evening."

"I don't like rain."

"Okay..."

"And I kind of run this world."

I guess that makes sense.

She adds, "Any particular reason you chose tonight with your weather at home?"

"I'm meeting Jennifer, actually."

"Oh, I see. I think I may know why."

"You do, of course. I really want to clear some things up with her and see if she will tell me the real reason that she's in this world with me."

"I understand. And if I can offer a little advice, just be patient. She will tell you eventually."

"I will. Thanks."

I snag the same circular table where Jennifer and I conversed the last time. Since I'm a little early, I take a moment to look around the room admiring the portraits on the wall of the greatness that came here before me.

"Eve?"

Jennifer approaches our table and greets me, leaning down with a side hug.

"Hello, Miss," I say to Jennifer now that she is in the seat across from me.

"What's up?" she asks me, knowing I have something on my mind.

"I've been thinking about this place and what you said about when you arrived."

"Yes?"

"I don't want to be disrespectful. I agree that saving a child is a huge deal, like I don't know if I could do it, but honestly, it's kind of your thing, you know? You're always at the hospital helping people."

"True."

"Just based on what Gina has been explaining to me

about this world, I feel like there's an even bigger reason why you're here."

"What could it be?" She looks interested in seeing if I know something.

"I have no idea. Are you keeping something from me?"

"Well, you are right. That's not the reason I'm here."

"I knew it."

Jennifer looks down at the table and exhales very loudly. Evidently, it's an even bigger reason than I can imagine.

"You don't have to tell me, Jennifer, it's alright. I'm just glad you're here; it doesn't matter why."

"No, it does, you're right. I want to tell you, but certainly no one except Gina knows."

"You know I'll just keep it to myself."

"I know." (She takes another deep breath.) "You were there for me when you took me to the clinic back at school when I thought I was sick and ended up pregnant."

"Of course, I remember. I was so worried about you."

"I know, and I should have told you then, but when I called Eric, he not only told me it wasn't his, he told me to get rid of it."

"What?!" I'm appalled, frustrated, and am suddenly back in the moment all over again.

"Yes. I mean I get he was angry but to just say to get

rid of it like it was no big deal, when in fact it's his child, was unbelievable to me. I mean you really find out who a person is in a difficult, unplanned situation."

"Isn't that the truth!"

"Obviously, I called my mom after that crying and telling her every single detail from feeling sick to the clinic reveal to Eric's response. After all of that, Mom told me that Eric wasn't entirely wrong or out of line."

"Really?"

"Can you believe it? My mother sent me numerous emails providing me with all of my options. She suggested we move to northern Carolina so no one would know I was pregnant then I could give the child up for adoption."

I know I don't have the right response, but my face shows how surprised I am by all of this.

"Did she tell you why she thought that?"

"She basically said that my life as a doctor would be over and the life of a single teenage mom would never be easy."

"So how did you get to the point where she became the main support system for you?"

"Well, when my dad, who I really don't speak to anymore, screamed at me and declared me an embarrassment, my mom chose the role of my biggest supporter. She and I went back and forth a lot, believe you me, but she eventually came around. And of course, I made the right decision for my life and for my daughter's."

"And did you ever hear from Eric again?"

"I texted him a few weeks after Annabelle was born to let him know that he was a father. I expected nothing from him, and I've heard nothing from him. Another bridge to cross when she is old enough to start asking about her father."

"So you don't know anything about what Eric's up to these days?"

"My guess is he's got another girl under his hooks. I don't know, nor do I care."

"Yea, neither does Melinda," I say under my breath.

"What?"

"You know Melinda is here?"

"Yea, I know her. Why would you say that?"

"The guy that screwed her over-my apologies for the choice of word-was Eric."

"What? Are you sure?"

"I am 99.9% sure!"

"Oh my gosh! I had no idea!"

"No one did!"

"Wow!" Jennifer mouthed while fiddling with her skirt. She had no idea.

"Jennifer, you certainly have showed great strength through everything. I'm so proud of you."

"Um, I'm so proud of you."

"My story isn't that impressive."

"But it's your story. You have chosen your own story to write."

"I like that."

"Well, thank you. Can I tell you something?"

"Of course. Anything!" Jennifer is all ears.

"I met someone."

"No way! Tell me about him."

"His name is Ben, and I actually met him at a bagel shop about a week ago."

"Where? Not like I would even know it."

"About a block away from the camp I'm working at this summer."

"What's he like?"

"He's very easy-going and very intelligent. He's from Boston."

"I wanna meet him!"

"You're the first person I've told about him."

"Nuh-uh."

"Yea-huh.

"Why?"

"I've only had breakfast with him, but we have a dinner date planned near the water next Friday night."

"Oh my gosh, that's so romantic."

"Isn't it?"

"You're beaming."

"I'm excited."

"Well, keep me posted."

"I will."

Jennifer stands up slowly, "My butt is asleep," she says. "I have to get back for bedtime."

"Oh, the life of a teen mom."

"Oh yes, you know they made a reality television show all about it. Call me after your date and thank you so much for being you."

"Ditto." We walk out together when Gina catches us halfway.

"Good night, girls."

"Good night, Gina," we respond in unison.

The rainstorm appears as soon as I approach the city. I love sleeping to the sound of rain, and tonight I intend to have very sweet dreams.

My World: Chapter Thirteen

I'm lying in bed the following morning when Jen texts at 7:15, a time I usually don't take phone calls, but I did just see her last night and I know she's excited we're together in both worlds.

Jen: Morning Eve. Sorry it's so early.

Eve: I'm only responding because it's you. What's going on?

Jen: I'm just so glad to have a friend in the alternate world that I can talk to.

Eve: I hear ya. Do you think we can be kicked out?"

Jen: What?

Eve: Like what if we do something that Gina doesn't like, and she makes us leave. I don't know if I could handle that.

Jen: Are you in some sort of trouble?

Eve: No.

Jen: So why would that idea even cross your mind?

Eve: I've just been thinking about everything. I re-

call Gina saying we're here for life but to make great decisions. I definitely got the feeling that I don't want to disappoint her.

Jen: I think you're good. I'll talk to you later. I hear someone calling my name.

I try and go back to sleep a little longer when my phone buzzes again.

Good morning, sunshine. It's Ben. I'm looking forward to Friday evening.

Who is this great guy? I wonder, still lying under the covers. He's bound to have something wrong with him. I just cannot imagine. I quickly text back **same here** then start feeling around the bedside table for my lip gloss.

Shoot! Where is my purse? Dammit, I left it at the mansion.

Thank goodness today does not have a tight schedule, but an added trip is certainly not on my agenda. What am I worried about? It won't take away any time from my day. I throw on some sweats and a top and roll out the door; I stop down the street for a cup of hot chocolate then hop on the bus-same route I've taken the last few days. I don't really want to talk to anyone, so I discreetly walk into the mansion and into the room where I was last night.

ALTERNATE WORLD

The tables are all bare, and my pink clutch is not in sight.

I'm sure there's a Lost and Found in here somewhere.

I start sneaking past the rooms looking for anything that could be a storage area for random articles of clothing. I walk past three rooms that are empty. No such luck. As I approach the fourth door, I notice it's cracked and dark, but candlelight is filling the room.

What's going on in there?

As quietly as I can possibly be, I stand still and place one eyeball through the crack. It's a circle of people chanting something. I notice Eve walking around the circle holding something in hand that she's motioning toward a girl in the middle of the circle.

I wonder.

I stare at the girl, who looks so familiar. She is crying and looking down at the floor while everyone else chants. Gina paces. I swear it looks like Rachel. I focus. It **is** Rachel.

I step forward ever so slightly and the floor creaks. I

wait a second to make sure no one has noticed me (thank goodness the ritual is in full swing in there). I continue to walk past like everything is normal and I didn't see a thing. I finally see a staff member I recognize.

"Good morning Eve," he says, "How can I help?"

"Do you all have a Lost and Found? I can't find my purse, and I'm pretty sure I left it here last night."

"Right this way, Miss." He leads me two doors down, which ends up being a giant closet of purses, jackets, scarves, anything you would expect to see in a Lost and Found except this was a walk-in closet that was organized and labeled from top to bottom.

"Wow! You can go shopping in here," I share.

"We prefer you don't," he responds curtly.

"I'm just kidding. That's my bag." I reach for the shelf third from the bottom. He waits for me to get it, then closes the door once my item has been retrieved.

"Anything else you need?" he asks.

"Nope. Thanks so much. I gotta run." And I escape out of the mansion without another hitch.

My World: Chapter Fourteen

I'm walking down the same path out when a call comes in from my sister. I send it to voicemail then listen to it on the bus.

Hey, sis. Gimme a call when you get this. I need your advice.

All I can think about on the ride home is the disturbing image coming from that room. I've never seen Gina so cross, and I know that was Rachel, but how have I never seen her here before. I'm definitely missing something.

When I get back to camp, I see a note on my cabin door that says **Meeting in Cafeteria.** I open the double doors to the cafeteria and see our head counselor giving direction for tomorrow. I saunter in and sit in the back so as not to interrupt her. One of the girls nods at me; I nod back and sit back to listen while my mind races. We receive the class roster for the new group starting tomor-row then head back to our respective areas to decorate for another arrival. Once I'm by myself I call my sister.

"Hey sis, what's going on?"

"Eve, I don't know what to do!"

"About what?"

"Sam proposed to me!"

"Wow! Congratulations!"

"You don't understand!"

"Then tell me."

"Sam moves to London after he graduates since he got a position at the largest publishing company there."

"And you have another year or so of school."

"Right."

"Well, you could do a long distance thing?"

"He doesn't want to do that."

"What does he want to do?"

"He wants me to go with him."

"What do you want to do?"

She doesn't answer, so I add, "He wants you to drop out of school?"

"He said that he will take care of me."

"Do you really think that's what you should do?"

"I don't know. I love him, and I don't want to lose him."

"If he loves you, he will wait for you."

"I knew you'd say that."

"It's true. What did Mom and Dad say? Did you tell them?"

"You were my first call."

"Good luck with that."

"Thanks."

All I can think is, *please make the right decision. Why does the guy always want you to give up your life for him?*

Evidently, Matt, Eric, and now Sam are all cut from the same cloth. I can only hope and pray that Ben is different, more like my father. Also, I want so badly for my sister to lead the life that she always dreamed about, and I know that living an ocean away from her family has never been a part of it. Only time will tell. I have to enjoy the peace and quiet today because the campers start back tomorrow, and they are a 24/7 job.

I'm standing outside of the cabin when the campers arrive bright and early Monday morning. One of the girls returned last week, so she helps me a lot by giving all of the information to the new campers. It makes my job a whole lot easier. In fact, this week feels much easier and flies by much faster than last week. It is Friday before we know it, and the campers are stuffing homemade picture frames and rock candy into their luggage to take home.

I'm especially glad it's Friday because it's my real first date with Ben. He offers to pick me up (the advantage of an older guy), so I'm waiting at the front of the camp when he comes in. I hardly want my closest friends to meet this guy, much less, some nosy summer camp counselors. Ever the gentleman though, Ben hops out of his car, with flowers in hand, at 5:30 on the dot, and comes around the passenger side to open my door.

"Hey Eve. You look great! I wanted us to be eating dinner while the sun is setting. Are you ready to go?"

"I am. This is perfect timing." He looks so cute in blue jeans with a blue button-down shirt with the sleeves rolled up to his elbows.

"I packed a variety of sandwich options, so hopefully we will have something that you like."

"I'm sure I will."

Ben looks at me with a smile saying, "I sure hope so. No pressure."

There is a brief silence before Ben starts asking about my summer job.

"How's it going, counselor?"

"I can say the same to you, counselor."

"Haha. Good one. I'm sure your position has a lot of more exciting stories. I'm in an office all day collecting research and organizing depositions for my dad and his team."

"Then yes, mine is way more fun. I hang out with elementary school and middle school girls and we sing, make smores, go swimming and kayaking, and do plenty of arts and crafts."

"I'm jealous." He smiles widely at me.

"Why are you jealous?"

"Because those girls get to spend more time with you than I do." I feel myself blush as I look toward the floor.

He pulls into the lot closest to the public park, opens up the trunk to remove a cooler and grocery bag and still manages to come open my door. I follow him down the sidewalk to the park; he puts down this cooler and removes a blanket from the bag before laying that on the grass. He spreads the towel out on the green then invites me to sit beside him. He brings out a cheese tray and a variety of drinks (water, juices, and soda).

"I should have asked you what you like to drink. Instead, I brought it all."

"Thank you. I'll just take a water for now."

"Cool. Me too."

Our conversation seems effortless. We discuss our families; he's an only child of an attorney father and author mother. We talk about school; he goes to the public school closest to Kerrington Prep but has some friends on campus with me. We even talk past relationships, which is easy because we both just have one that really wasn't that dramatic. *(What a relief!)* It wasn't until I started getting cold around 8:00 that we pack up everything and head to the car. Neither one of us is ready for the date to end, but it is freezing.

"We can finish this at my house if you'd like?" he asks reluctantly, "We have wine there, and my parents are at a benefit for a few more hours.

"I'd love to."

A smile plasters across my face as we climb back into the car. He drives cautiously, left hand on the wheel, right hand hovering around the gear close to my leg. Back at his place, we get comfortable on the couch picking up the conversation right where we left off.

"Can I make you a drink? We have beer, wine, liquor, whatever you want."

"I'm okay. Thanks."

"I guess I'm okay too, since I do need to get you back to work in one piece."

"That would be much appreciated." I take a swig of water.

He gets up for a moment to turn on some music then joins me back on the sofa much closer than he was before. Without saying a word, Ben leans in and kisses me on the mouth. It's quick and sweet, but he has the softest lips and I only want to try again. Clearly, he feels the same because he leans in again but this time gently moving me until I'm lying flat on my back and he's on top of me. The rhythm of our bodies together is perfectly in sync with the music playing in the background. Not wanting this to be my first and last memory with Ben, I kind of shimmy myself up.

"Are you okay?" His voice is soft and concerning.

"Yea. Do you know what time it is?"

"It's almost 9. What's the matter?"

"I think I should be getting back to camp."

"Okay. I'll take you there."

"Thank you."

"No problem. Let me run to the bathroom then we're off."

I stand in the front hall second guessing myself. *Maybe I shouldn't have come back to his house. Maybe I gave him the wrong impression.*

Ben walked toward me like nothing had happened.

"Are you ready to go?" he asks. I nod yes, and that was it-my cue saying this would be my first and last date with Ben.

"After you," he politely motions before he locks the front door then for the final time, opens the car door for me. He starts the car and turns on the radio as we quietly listen to the lyrics of Dua Lipa. It feels like it's taking forever to get back to camp. Finally, he breaks the awkwardness at the red light.

"I want to see you again." He casually puts his hand on my leg and kisses me on the cheek.

"I'd like that."

A feeling of pleasure, content, and relief take over my body. I really want to be with Ben; I can only imagine every single day being better than the last. I know that he's the one that will make me happy. Since it's the weekend, we make plans to meet tomorrow morning for breakfast at a nearby breakfast spot.

"I'll pick you up at 10."

"Sounds good," I say as I leap out of his car and down the sidewalk to my cabin.

The hole in the wall breakfast spot has wooden booths lining the walls and smells of eggs and bacon as soon as you open the door.

"Hey, Ben," the host says, "Sit wherever you'd like. I'll get you some menus."

"Come here often?" I laugh.

"I love convenience, but you will love the food. The pancakes are the best."

I'm scanning the menu when a female appears at the head of the table. Unexpectedly, it's not our server.

"Erin? What are you doing here?"

"I was going to call you today. I arrived last night with my mom. You know my mom's cousin lives here, right? She's in assisted living."

"Is she okay?"

"She has Alzheimer's."

"I'm sorry."

"Thanks. My mom is in the car. I ran in here to pick up some bagels to go."

"Well, this is actually my first time eating here myself. Erin, this is Ben. Ben, this is Erin. She and I grew up together; she lives back home in Virginia."

Erin smiles, and Ben extends his hand. "A pleasure to meet you, Erin," he politely says.

"Likewise. Enjoy your breakfast. Talk to you later, Eve."

"When do you go back home?"

"Later tonight- a direct flight back."

Sounds good, girl. I'll call you. Give your mom a hug for me."

"Will do!" she yells as she's running out the door.

"Are you ready to order?" The server appears and asks.

"I'm going to try the chocolate chip pancakes," I say.

"Same here," Ben says before handing over the menus. Once she has walked out of earshot, he adds, "I'm so glad to know you love chocolate" and winks.

"I'm sure." I smile back flirtatiously. I look down at the table waiting for the silence to be filled.

"Do you want to go to a movie tonight?" he asks.

"I would love to."

"I'll pick you up at 6:00."

"Perfect."

"Here you go." The server arrives, her hands full with both platters. "Enjoy."

"Thank you, " we respond in unison.

After breakfast, Ben drives me back to camp.

"Thanks for the pancakes. I'll be ready at 6."

Once on the freeway, I call Erin.

"Erin, it's Eve. I'm so sorry that I didn't know you

were in town this week. Are you and your mom with your aunt?"

"Yes."

"I'd love to stop by and visit longer."

"That would be great, but how will you get here?"

"I'll take the bus. See you soon."

I take a shower then change into something that is casual enough hang with Erin and hot enough to make Ben want to call me again.

Chapter Fifteen

Erin is waiting for me in the lobby when I arrive and jumps up to hug me.

"Eve, thank you for meeting me!"

"Of course, twice in one day, and you don't even live here."

"Yea, really. How crazy was that?"

"I like Ben," Erin blurts out.

I blush before saying, "Do you really?"

"I do; he's adorable. I'm kind of jealous."

"Whatever."

"No, really, I went out with hottest black guy for a few months at home but didn't tell anyone about it. I was too afraid my parents would be mad."

"Erin, have you not learned that you have to live your life for you, not your parents?"

"I know. I'm working on it. If Ben has a brother or a cousin, keep me in mind."

"I know he doesn't have a brother, he's an only child, but I can work on the cousin thing. He's pretty great."

"He seems it." Erin and I just hang out for few hours before she and her mom have to head to the airport.

"Do you want us to take you somewhere?" Erin asks.

"Let me think where we are in relation to the airport." I pause a moment then continue, "You know what, if you can drop me off on the way, that would be great."

"Of course, we will," Erin's mom responds, "You are a true friend to come visit us today. I'm sorry we didn't plan better, but it was kind of a family emergency."

"I understand."

They drop me off a few blocks from camp, and she adds, "We'll be sure to tell your mother we saw you and what a lovely daughter she has raised."

"Thank you. Safe travels home."

I had turned my phone off at the nursing home, and when I turn it back on, I see it's already 5:50. I have four missed calls from Ben on my cell phone. I quickly call him back.

He answers on the first ring. "Eve, where have you been? Are you okay? I've been trying you for hours."

"I'm okay. Sorry Ben, I ended up spending the afternoon with Erin. I turned my phone off."

"That's fine. I was just worried since I hadn't heard from you since you left after breakfast."

"Aww, that's sweet. I'm great, and I'll be ready for you at 6."

"See you in ten minutes, beautiful."

Ben pulls in right on time, and I hop in the car.

"Hi, Eve. So, the movie isn't until 7:30, but I figured we could grab some appetizers right near the theater. Are you hungry?

"Starving actually. I just realized I haven't had a thing to eat since breakfast."

The restaurant is dark inside; we grab a high-top table. Our legs touch while we order, talk, laugh, and eat. I realize at this moment that I think I'm falling in love with Ben. Is that even possible so quickly? We go to the movie, which isn't that great, but the company to my right is ideal. We sat in the very back row where he pulled me close to him the entire time and found a way to kiss my cheek, neck, and mouth throughout the film.

He asked to walk me to my cabin. How can I refuse his gorgeous face? When I see the coast is clear, I unlock my cabin door and pull him in behind me. Leaning against the closed door, he starts kissing my neck which quickly turns into his tongue inside my mouth. He lifts his arms up, and I pull his shirt over his head. We fall onto the floor, him on top of me, my arms holding onto his caramel body. I know he doesn't want to hear what I have to say, which is that this can't happen here. Our timing is horrible.

"Ben!" I loudly whisper between breaths until he hears me and stops.

"What?" He whispers back.

"Don't be mad, but you can't stay here. We can't do this here. In fact, you shouldn't even be in here now."

"You're kidding me, right?"

"I know. I'm so sorry. Believe me. I don't want you to go either, but I need this job."

"And I need you," he manages to get out as he passionately kisses my earlobes and neck.

"You gotta go," I say pushing him off of me and stand up myself. He puts on his shirt and follows me to the door. I open a crack to see if anyone is out there.

"Go now," I command, and I watch him walk to his car as calmly as possible like nothing happened while I try to get some composure and attempt to get some sleep. I must have slept with a permanent grin on my face because it is still there when I awaken the next morning. A text appears on my phone.

Ben: Good morning Eve.

"It is a good morning indeed," I say aloud and text back.

Ben: What are you doing today?
Eve: It's Sunday, so we are preparing for the final session of camp. What about you?
Ben: Thinking about you.
Eve: That's sweet.
Ben: It's true. I'll probably go to the gym a few hours. You don't think anyone saw us last night, right?"

Eve: I think we were good, but that was close.
Ben: It was worth it. Until next time….
Eve: Bye.

ALTERNATE WORLD

It's Sunday. Maybe Rachel comes to the mansion on Sundays. I have got to find out if that was her. *What time is it?* It's worth a shot. I wander in the mansion looking as casual as possible; I should have purposefully left something here last time so I would have a better excuse to return. What am I saying? Gina says I'm always welcome here; I'm acting paranoid. I need to act like myself and not like I'm trying to uncover some giant secret. I'm walking around the living room smiling at people passing by when I swear, I see Ellie and Justin on the other side of the room. I haven't seen anyone from back home in here before. Is that really them?

Gina glides into the room moments later and I motion her over.

"Gina, do you have a moment? I have a few questions."

"Of course, dear. How are you this fine Sunday? What's on your mind?"

"Do you know them?"

"Who are you referring to darling?"

"That couple over there. Is that Ellie? "

"Yes."

"Ellie went to high school with me, and I think that's her on again, off again boyfriend, Justin."

"You are correct, but they are definitely on again."

"What are they doing here?"

"What do you mean?"

"Like, how are they in the alternate world?"

"Just like you are in the alternate world. They are in the alternate world."

"Oh my gosh!" I shout aloud.

"What?" Gina asks concerned.

"Justin is in a wheelchair."

"Yes, he is."

"What happened to him?"

"Sadly, he was in a motorcycle accident; his legs are permanently paralyzed."

My mind goes blank for a minute then I remember Erin saying she saw them before. I tell Gina.

"Wait! My friend Erin said she saw Ellie and Justin arguing on a street corner back home. She saw Justin ahead of her and Ellie following screaming and crying. What happened?

"That was the tragic day. Justin borrowed his step-brother's motorcycle for the day and wanted to surprise Ellie. She didn't want to ride it and begged him not to either. He walked away from her, hopped on the bike, and was run off the road just a few miles later by an SUV."

"Oh, my gosh. That's horrible. Are they in here together?"

"They are. Ellie got a call from Justin's stepbrother after the accident and she went directly to the hospital; she missed a lot of school staying by his side. I am a fan of true love, and I don't see it very often, especially at this young age, but these two love each other against all odds. They will be together for the long haul. Wherever one goes, the other follows. This is not the life they would have planned for, but they are in it together. They are both back in school planning a future together."

"Wow. I think I'll wait a while to say hi," Eve says.

"It's your call, but it is always nice to see a friendly face.

"Are there other couples in here, Gina?"

"Let me think. I know we've had some here in the past, but they're hard to come by nowadays."

"Why is that?"

"So often in a relationship, someone has compromised something or altered a plan of their own for the sake of the other individual. They usually keep it to themselves to the grave."

"That's so sad."

"Oh, it is. I hate knowing some people are giving up

their happiness for someone else to get their own happiness. Imagine the possibilities when people are happy together for each other and themselves."

"That's what I want."

"And you shall find it, if that's what you want."

"What if I'm dating someone? Can I tell him about this place?"

"Most women or men who try to tell their significant other about our alternate world, usually come here upset. Many of our members tell us that their partner thinks they are lying or are totally delusional. I get it. It's a tricky situation. Many people can't believe something they can't see. At first, the partner may seem supportive but become extra cautious around the other. They start withholding information and acting very suspicious."

"How can you be in a relationship and not tell each other everything?"

"Honey, most couples don't tell each other everything. It's good to keep a little mystery and things to yourself, especially about your past."

"I guess so. I want to be honest, but I don't want Ben to think I'm crazy."

"Less is more, dear, always."

Gina walks away, and I don't see a sign of Rachel there at all. I guess that little ceremony is not a weekly occurrence. I turn around to take one more look at Ellie and Justin. They are in a corner nuzzling each other with grins on both of their faces. They do look happy, and Gina says that's the ultimate goal. I gather my belongings to exit for the day and return to begin the final week of summer camp.

My World: Chapter Sixteen

Once in the clearing to the camp, my phone registers two missed calls, one from Ben and one from my sister. *What time is it? What time did they call? Note to self,* I say aloud, *there is no cell phone tower in the alternate world. I don't know why I never noticed that before.* I try to wrap my brain around this deal.

I'm not really living two different lives; this is just one part of my life that I cannot share (difficult but not impossible). I will have to remember to make up an excuse if anyone starts asking where I am when they call me. I don't want people suspecting something. It's not like it impacts anyone; no time is lost when I'm gone. Easy. I decide to call my sister back first.

"Hey Sis, it's Eve!"

"Eve, Did Mom and Dad tell you?"

"Tell me what?"

"I'm getting married!"

"You're what?"

"I'm getting married!"

"I heard you, but I'm confused."

"I thought I had mentioned it before."

"Last time we talked, you said he asked you to get married, but you were seriously debating what to do."

"Right, and I decided to move to London. We're getting married in three months."

"What did Mom and Dad say?"

"They told me not to rush into these things and I have my whole life ahead of me and what kind of job can I get these days without a college degree and blah, blah, blah...."

"They are right, you know?"

"Please don't side with them. I need the support of my maid-of-honor."

"Me?"

"Last time I checked, you were my only sister."

"And I am thrilled to be your maid-of-honor, but I really only want to do that once."

"I can't believe you just said that!"

"I'm sorry, Hope. I do want to support you and if this is really what you want, I'm here for you."

"Thanks, Eve. I'll call you later! We have lots of planning to do!

"Looking forward to it!"

No, not my sister. Is my sister going to be one of those unfortunate ones who gives up on her own dreams? And what happened to my mom and dad too? I can't tell if the pit in my stomach is hunger or anxiety, but I pop a bag of micro-wave popcorn just the same and lay out on my bed. I have just a few more hours of quiet time before the campers arrive. The weeks have really flown by. Engrossed in my reality TV, I hardly notice my phone beeping informing me I have at least a few texts. And they are all from Ben.

Ben: I miss you. I'd love to make dinner for you next weekend. Meet me at my house at 7PM on Saturday. Just bring your beautiful self.

Eve: You cook? That sounds intriguing. I actually head home for the rest of the summer next Sunday, so Saturday would be great, but can you pick me up? I'll be at the camp.

Ben: I cook pasta. Don't get too excited. How about I pick you up at 6PM then and you can help me finish making dinner.

Eve: How romantic!

I fall sound asleep and wake up to the dinging of my phone alarm; I dress in my camp counselor gear and stand at attention outside of the door to greet the new arrivals. When I see their huge smiles and hear high shrieks, I forget how this is the first day for so many these kiddos. I've been here three weeks, so it all feels old hat to me. I plaster a big smile on my face and welcome all of the girls with a hug. Then, kayaking, horseback riding, pottery class, and meals in the cafeteria begin. I get all the kids situated in their bunks then check the voicemail left by Mom.

Hi Eve, I'm sure you have heard about your sister's upcoming day this fall. And I know she wants her sister to be a part of all of the festivities. Dad will pick you up from the airport next Sunday. We will plan the shower, rehearsal dinner, and wedding all the same week so people can just come in once to participate before she moves. I look forward to seeing you, honey, and your sister does too. Call me later. Love you!

Of course, I don't call her later. I jump into camp counselor mode. Each day, we add another adventure to the list and share another meal together. The days turn into nights and the final week is the fastest one yet. On Friday afternoon, we put on our weekly performance for the parents, complete with chants, raps, songs, gymnastics, and popping. We wave goodbye to the families from the top of the hill then gather in the cafeteria for our counselor dinner and reception. It's weird to think that come tomorrow this will all be over, and I'll be at home for the rest of summer vacation. It also means I will be far away from Ben after one more night together. I pack my bags then meet up with some of the counselors in the theater for a movie night. It's almost two in the morning before we call it a night.

Since I didn't set the alarm, I roll over at 11:00 in the morning. I pull the sheets off all of the beds in the cabin then meet the gang for a final lunch in the cafeteria. I find some chocolate chip cookie dough and decide to make some cookies for Ben. I have enough time in the day to say farewell to my staff. I shower and get dressed in a pencil skirt and black tank top, casual but cute-perfect for a night I'm sure to remember. Always the punctual one, Ben drives the road at six on the dot. He looks so good in his khaki shorts and pale blue polo shirt. He comes to my cabin and helps carry my luggage to the car. I close the cabin door, follow behind him, and stop at the trunk with my plate of cookies in hand.

"These are for you," I say.

"I said you didn't have to bring a thing but yourself."

"I know, but I'm a southern girl. You can't go to anyone's home empty handed."

"That's nice."

"Anyway, they are just chocolate chip cookies. You can keep them to eat later."

"Or we can have them together for dessert."

"That sounds good too." I blush. He places the cookies in the trunk beside my bags then he opens the door for me like the gentleman he is. During the drive, I realize that I have never even seen his home in the light before. And when we arrive, it is breathtaking! It's a totally different house from the last one. This home sits up on a bluff with the water in the background.

"This is where you live?" The shock is evident in my voice.

"This is my family's lake house. They gave me the key for the weekend."

"They let you stay here by yourself?"

"It is our home, and I have stayed home alone before. Haven't you?"

Embarrassed, I say, "Yes. I have. I guess, technically during the school year, I am on my own."

"Well, there you go." So, I hope you like Cappellini."

"I love it."

"Well then, come on into the kitchen and make yourself at home. I will get your bags."

"Thank you so much! Your home is beautiful."

"Thank you, I like it!"

I'm sitting at his kitchen bar while he chops vegetables, stirs the noodles, and adds seasoning to the sauce. He's definitely done this before. We enjoy small talk when my phone rings. When I see my mother's name on the id, I let it go to voice mail then listen to it.

"Sorry, I need to take this." I hop off the stool and fumble with my phone.

"No problem." He glances up at me then adds, "Take your time."

I wander into the living room and listen to the message.

Hi Eve, it's Mom again. I realize you have had a busy week with summer camp, but we need to talk about the upcoming plans for your sister. Let me know your flight information tomorrow. Call me back. Love you!

I've never been able to hide my expression, which I guess Ben could tell since he stops stirring to ask me what is wrong when I return to the kitchen. I just start blurting out information, which I can hardly decode myself.

"That was my mom. My sister is getting married in three months."

"That's exciting."

"That's not all. The guy she's marrying is moving to London and wants her to move with him immediately."

"Well, isn't that usually how it happens?"

"The thing is, he wants her to drop out of college to be with him. He says he'll take care of her."

"Well, that's nice. Do they love each other?" *What a weird response for a guy.*

"I don't know. But she's giving up on her own dreams and aspirations just to follow this guy."

"Is that what you think or did she say that?"

"She hasn't, but I know this was never her plan."

"Sometimes people's plans don't always work out."

"Yes, but you have to work for it."

"Is your life going as planned?"

"Not at all." *I can't believe I just said that out loud. The images of the alternate world just filled my mind.*

"So, it's better than you thought or worse than you imagined?"

"I don't want to jinx myself, but it's different from what I always thought my life would be, but so far I'm loving it."

"There you go. I think you should hear your sister out."

"Okay, can we eat now?" I'm done with this conversation and ready for a distraction.

"Of course! You fill the glasses and I'll make the plates."

"Fill the glasses with what?" I ask.

"My parents always have beer and wine in the fridge."
"I'll just have water." I respond.

"Are you sure? I'm going to have a beer."

"You are?"

"We aren't going anywhere. Help yourself."

I hesitantly remove two cold Coronas from the refrigerator and pour them into the tall glasses.

Dinner is delightful, but my mind is not entirely in the moment, and I feel bad since he has clearly gone out of his way to create this romantic evening.

"Ben, this dinner is amazing. I'm sorry I'm not really talkative. I know you have gone out of your way."

"You're great, and I understand. Believe me. All families go through ups and downs. I'm sure it will work out."

"I'm thinking I may need someone to be with me at this family event....what do you think?"

"I'd love to be there for you. Just tell me when."

"Really? You really don't even know me."

"I know you well enough."

"Okay then, I will let you know!"

I kiss him across the table and thank him again for dinner. He hops up to take the dishes to the sink then I notice he returns with two glasses of red wine.

"Shall we head to the sofa? Maybe we can get to know each other a little better."

I take his hand and follow him to the den; he sits down on the couch and motions for me to sit right beside him before he turns on the television for background noise. I nervously sip my wine and feel Ben staring at me. When I glance back at him, he pushes the hair out of my face and tells me how beautiful I am. He obviously feels comfortable with me because he turns to stretch his body out and rests his head in the middle of my lap. We watch a little TV, rub each other's hair, and kiss for the rest of the night before we fall asleep in the same position on the couch. The sun shines bright in the window around 7 in the morning, which causes us both to stir. Ben starts kissing me again on the mouth then on the neck, and I get caught up in the moment all over again. After about ten minutes, he stands up and asks what I want for breakfast. I take the time to freshen up in the bathroom and call my mom. I dial our home number.

"Hello," my dad answers.

"Hey Dad!"

"Hello, my little Eve! How are you?"

"I'm fine. Is Mom there?"

"She sure is. Are you ready to come back home and plan the Thompson wedding?"

"Yes, my flight is currently on time."

"Very good. You keep me posted, and I'll be there to pick you up this evening. Your mom won't tell you this, but she definitely could use your help when you get here."

"I know, Dad. I will."

"That's my girl. Now, let me get your mom."

Dad puts his hand over the receiver before screaming out to my mom, who must be upstairs since a few minutes pass before she gets on the phone.

"Hi Eve, did you get my message?"

"Yes, that's why I'm calling."

"Mom, is this wedding really happening so quickly?"

"Yes. Isn't this exciting? We will host the shower the Thursday before the wedding and of course the rehearsal dinner will be Friday."

"A wedding weekend in the fall."

"It will be lovely, darling! I'm excited to hear what's going on in your new life too."

You have no idea is all I want to say.

"Thanks Mom! See you soon!

Ben was scraping scrambled eggs from the frying pan on our plates when I joined him in the kitchen.

"How's your family?"

"My mom is over the moon about my sister's wedding. I have a feeling that's all she will be talking from here on out."

"One day she'll be talking all about your wedding, Eve."

"I guess you're right."

"How did you sleep?"

"Good, how about you?"

"I slept great! Now, eat up! What time should we leave for the airport?"

"My flight leaves at 4:00."

"Okay, it's about an hour fifteen from here, so let's leave in about thirty."

"Sounds good."

I'm glad we have a little more time together before we are apart for at least a month. We chat, hold hands, and sing top 40 hits during the road trip. When we arrive at the airport, Ben hops out to get my luggage before he gives me a huge hug and long kiss.

"I'll miss you, Eve Thompson."

"I'll miss you too, Ben Parker."

"Call me when you land."

"I will."

As I walk through security, I start thinking about home and everything I have missed this year alongside everything that has happened to me this year. It's a lot to digest. Hopefully the fifty-five-minute flight home will help me process it all.

Chapter Seventeen

Dad is right on time, as always, to pick me up at the airport. I see him right away. *Just seeing my dad makes me want to spill everything. It's hard enough keeping the alternate world from Ben, but my dad knows everything about me. How can I keep it to myself?*

"Welcome home, darling."

"Thanks, Dad. I can't believe it's summer already."

"We are so glad you're home. What color is your suitcase, Eve?" Dad asks while leading the way to the carousel.

"Blue and green polka dots."

We watch a few bags go by before I struggle to haul mine off.

"I can't believe that is under twenty-five pounds."

"You got it?"

"Yep, let's go."

He carries my bag and asks if I'm hungry. *I'm always hungry.* He informs me that Mom is out with friends, so he and I do dinner together at our favorite neighborhood pub. I'm so tired (for reasons I can't really share with parents), so after dinner I take a shower and visit with Mom a bit before I head to bed. After a much-needed slumber, I text Erin.

Hey girl! I'm home! Do you have plans today? My mind has been racing and I want to run it by you.

Erin responds that she can meet me at the coffee shop down the street in ten minutes, which is perfect since I haven't eaten a thing this morning and I can walk there. Running out the door, I tell Mom I'm meeting Erin for breakfast and will be back later. Erin is already at the table with two hot teas and a muffin in hand.

"Good morning, Erin."

"Hey, Eve! Welcome home."

"Thanks, girl. Glad to be home."

"We have so much to catch up on."

"Don't I know it! So, what's up, Eve?"

"I know this is going to sound of the blue, but do you remember Rachel?"

"Rachel, Ellie's friend?"

"Yea, but they are not friends anymore."

"Really?"

"A lot can happen in a year. What made you think about her anyway?"

"I was thinking about our seventh-grade dance. Remember, she went with us then left to go with what's his name?"

"Kevin- "

"What?"

"His name was Kevin."

"Oh right! She didn't sleep with Kevin that night and found her way to the after party."

"Yes, and?"

"Do you remember what she was talking about that following Monday morning at school? She came running over to tell us about a lady in a pink dress and a magical house and all of that!"

After seeing Rachel in the mansion a few weeks ago, I'm trying to make sure my mind isn't playing tricks on me. If anyone can help me sort out this story, it's Erin. She's so logical.

"Oh, I remember! Rachel was such an attention seeker. She totally made that up thinking we wouldn't talk about the actual incident."

"You really think that?"

"Of course, wasn't she going off about some mysterious world or something?"

"Yes, I think so." *I suddenly try not to sound too interested.*

"She's so weird. Now, fill me in on everything starting with the beautiful Ben you introduced me to earlier this year."

"He's still great. We spent the night together on Saturday."

"No way! Did anything happen?"

"Everything and nothing at all."

"It sounds amazing."

"He is."

"How long are you here for?"

"Until mid-August when school resumes."

"Good! I've missed you."

"I've missed you too. I promised my dad I'd help my mom, so I'm headed back, but thanks for meeting me. I'll see you later."

"Later girl."

Mom is at home doing laundry, so I ask her if she wants my help. I know I'll be otherwise occupied again later tonight, so I need to stay around the house and try to find a way to sneak out tonight. I've never visited the mansion from anywhere but from Boston, so I don't even know if it's possible, but if Rachel was telling the truth, it can happen for sure. I've got to meet Gina at the mansion at 8:00 tonight.

Mom and I spend most of the day straightening up around the house, comparing stories from school to home, and then cooking dinner for the three of us. Dad joins us to enjoy Mom's famous lasagna. Just like old times, we sit around the table and talk about our day-no cell phones at the dinner table. (Quite the opposite of my school dining hall.)

"I'm going to meet up with Erin tonight."

"Didn't you just see her this morning?" Mom responds.

"Yes, but I haven't seen her in months."

"You haven't seen us in months either."

Dad chimes in, "She's living here for the next few months. A visit with Erin this evening will be fine."

"Thanks Dad."

"No problem, kiddo. Just help us clean the kitchen before you go."

"I will. I'll be back."

ALTERNATE WORLD

Since it's so light out, I start walking down the sidewalk toward the big intersection when the four-lane road miraculously turns into the clearing I know now so well.

"You look like you're here on a mission," Gina shouts as I run up the front steps.

"Do you have a minute?" I ask.

"Well sure, come on in."

I follow behind the boss lady to a private room, a small dark oval shaped room big enough for a round table and four chairs with new portraits hanging on the wall. Gina motions me to sit down.

"So, shoot!" she shouts.

"I don't know how to start exactly. I went to junior high school with a girl named Rachel."

"Rachel who?"

"Rachel Winston," I interject.

"Ahh, yes, Rachel." Her tone changes and her smile quickly disappears.

I hesitate then continue, "She was a friend of Ellie's."

I'm so nervous I can't stop talking."

"You know Ellie," I add, "She is in this world, actually, with her boyfriend Justin."

Gina sounds a little fed up when she says, "Yes, yes. I know Ellie. So, what does she have to do with Rachel?"

"Rachel joined our group to our spring dance over a year ago and had an altercation with a guy from our class before returning back to our group later."

"I see...." Gina remarks. It is evident that already knows this story, so I feel the details are not that necessary, but of course she is not offering any additional information.

I add, "Then that Monday at school, she confided in us that a lady all dressed in pink helped her when her car broke down and brought her to a mansion."

"Did you believe her?"

"We really didn't' think much of it at the time. We didn't know her very well."

"That's right," Gina states. "Did she tell you anything else?"

"Not really," I reply, "She kept telling us she felt like she was in a dream but knew it wasn't but couldn't process it."

"And she swore us not to tell anyone else," I respond.

"She wasn't supposed to tell anyone at all," Gina firmly answers. "You know the rules."

"I do," I softly say.

I ask, "So is she here?"

I'm wondering if she will confirm the fact that I did see Rachel a few weeks ago in some sort of weird intervention. Gina was there.

"No. She's no longer here."

"Why not?"

"She chose a different path."

"What do you mean?" I ask anxiously then watch Gina breathe deeply before she answers.

"Rachel was a sweet girl and one of our youngest members. We rarely get any junior high schoolers. It's a very vulnerable group of individuals. Well, Rachel was different and such an example to follow. Unfortunately, she didn't carry on that same path in tenth grade. She became confused with her life and succumbed to peer pressure. She didn't just experiment with drugs; she became addicted to everything from pot to cocaine. We tried everything we could to help her in here, but she wasn't open. She was released from here. I've been watching from a distance, and I believe she has finally checked into rehab at home this summer."

"Oh my gosh!" I cry out, "No wonder she and Ellie don't speak anymore."

"Yes, it's very sad, but like I told you all, you can't use this world as an escape. What you do in the real world translates here."

"And that's what Rachel did?" I question.

"Why yes, she thought she could do drugs in the real world and come here to feel peace. She was on a path to greatness. But these two worlds collide, and she was no exception. She wasn't true to herself because she was trying too hard to fit in and she became someone unrecognizable.

"And there's nothing you could do?" I was pleading on her behalf.

"Quite the opposite. We did everything we could do."

"But she is going to go to rehab?" I inquire.

"Not on her own, I'm afraid to say. Only after she was dismissed from here."

"Wow!" I'm truly speechless.

"Yes, it's sad but true. If we allow everyone to use the alternate world as their safe haven with no consequences for their actions, then we are not the unique destination we have created for deserving individuals like you. Is that all you wanted to know about?"

"Yes, thank you Gina," I say.

"Well, if you will excuse me," Gina says as she stands up from our table. "I can only hope this conversation helps you as you grow as an individual in both worlds. It was too much for Rachel. I hope it won't be too much of a burden for you. It is a privilege, and we want to help you become the person you dream of becoming. I've seen the future, Eve, and it looks very bright for you."

I stay seated and stunned. I am in disbelief. I'm sitting in the same place that Rachel was talking about over a year ago when we thought she was delusional. Now, she's not even around to talk to about it. I don't even know where to find her; Erin doesn't even know where she can be. I stand up and glance around the room looking for last minute answers before I leave. I exit the house and walk out of the clearing where it is still light on the main highway home. I walk in the door and hear mom's voice shout out from the kitchen.

My World: Chapter Eighteen

"That was fast! Did you forget something?"

"What do you mean?" I ask confused.

"You just left about a minute ago." I quickly remember how time does not move on earth at the same speed as in the alternate world, so I come up with an excuse.

"Oh yea, Erin and I just decided it was getting dark and to meet up later this week."

"Well, you can join your dad and me in the den. We're putting on the movie at 8." I jump on the couch beside my dad and pull my phone from my pocket to search for Rachel Winston.

The next few weeks are pretty much how it used to be; my time is balanced between home and friends. In fact, I'm so into this world that I realize I haven't talked to Jen or even visited the alternate world for a while. And that is fine with me right now; things are making sense and I'm in a good place. It's a surreal feeling to be living your life and planning your day-to-day while understanding through the alternate world-ultimately your destiny. By the time I'm forty-five, I'll be a well-known lawyer to powerful females. I'm just hoping my daily decisions successfully match this path. What happens if they don't?

What would my life be like if I had given in to Matt and created my world around him and his needs? No, that's no way to live. Things are as they should be. My phone dings, and a text arrives from Ben.

Hey babe, this week is crazy for me as I'm headed up to the Cape in the morning with my family. I miss you and will call you when I return. XOXO-Ben

Thank goodness my mom keeps me busy. She and I head out to go shopping. I need at least two new dresses for Hope's events. Hopefully I can get some new back to school items as well. Mom also wants to hit Crate and Barrel to start Hope's registry. Who knows how long that will take? I'm meandering up and down the rows of wine glasses and bath towels and realize that I just want to talk to Jennifer. She is spending a lot of her time in the alternate world, mainly because she wants to talk to Melinda and find out her side of the story.

Melinda is always so quiet, often keeping to herself, but apparently Jennifer manages to get her to say hello when they pass each other on the grounds. Jennifer has been drawn to Melinda knowing there was something that connects them, and she wanted to see if Melinda felt it too. She finally caught up to her one day after at least eight days in a row of casually stalking her. Afterward, she told me she's dying to tell me what she'd learned. I call her while Mom is busily examining every item on the kitchen aisle. She answers on the first ring.

"Jen!"

"Hey, Eve! How are you?"

"Good. I'm back at home for the summer. I've been dying to hear what's going on."

"Here goes. I finally got to introduce myself and ask Melinda to lunch. She was hesitant, but agreed, and we picked out a table in the mansion dining room. She asked how I knew her. I told her I went to Kerrington for a semester and I know you did too, so I kind of wanted to see if we knew the same people."

"Good one, Jen!"

"I thought so, but she just said *small world, but I doubt it, it's a pretty big campus.*"

"Hmmm." I'm processing her reply.

"I told her she'd be surprised and asked her if she ever hung out at a particular place, and she said she really kept to herself. I asked some probing questions to which she didn't budge. When I asked her if she ever went to parties at Ryan's house, she started talking."

"And what did she say?" I eagerly ask while trying to keep my voice relatively low since I'm still in the store.

"She said that during her first year, she did hang out

there. I told her my ex-boyfriend was on the basketball team and always at those parties. Of course, she asked his name and I stumbled over my words before I just said, *His name is Eric.*"

"Melinda took a swig of her tea when I noticed her eyes started filling up with tears. I asked her if she was okay, and she said she didn't want to say anything about my boyfriend. I assured her that whatever she said couldn't be any worse than what I've said about him. Then she just whispered, *Eric attacked me.*"

"She did?"

"Yes, you were right."

There was a silent pause before she continued.

"Melinda said she had gone to several parties there and that Eric had chatted her up on several visits. She said that one night she noticed he was a little agitated and more drunk than usual, but she liked him, so she went with him in the laundry room. One thing led to another which ended up in yelling before she slipped out from under him, unlocked the laundry room door, and ran out of the house."

"That's just awful!" I explain.

"I know. I asked her when it happened, and she said it was in the beginning of spring semester. I was back home then."

"That's right. Jen, did you tell her?"

"I told her I dropped out before spring semester began because I got pregnant. She put her hand on her mouth and said, "Don't tell me." I nodded and said, *Yes, Eric is my baby's father, but he will never admit it to anyone else. I never heard from him again. He doesn't even know he now has a baby daughter.*"

"Anything else you learned today? Like this wasn't enough already." I laugh.

"Actually, she proceeded to tell me that Eric started awful rumors about her, so she moved back home to attend a local private school. She asked me if I knew what had become of Eric and I assured her he was not in the alternate world. We laughed, hugged, and said we'd meet again. I want you to be there too."

"Let's make it happen girl. I gotta run. Mom is giving me the evil eye."

"Talk to you later."

I am so busy at home over summer break with Mom, Dad, and friends that I communicate with Ben only through text. The advantage of dating long-distance is you really don't have to explain your day because you're both busy doing your own thing. This week is pretty much the same story except that I am meeting Jen at 7 p.m.. tonight at the mansion.

ALTERNATE WORLD

I leave around 6:30 and walk the majestic path to Gina's house. While on the way, I realize I haven't been for a while, then wonder if I should make more of an effort to balance the two worlds. It is a privilege to have this opportunity. When I walk in this evening, it is more somber than usual. People are standing in the hallway leaving flowers underneath one of the gigantic paintings. I spot Gina at the center of it all and meander my way through the circle to reach her. *I've definitely missed something.*

"Gina, what's going on?" I feverishly whisper to her.

"We lost one of the greats today."

"Who?"

"Mr. William Grant from London, England. He was a powerful member of Parliament who truly cared for the people."

"I never met him," I softly say.

"His spirit remains with us forever, but I know his family on earth is suffering today."

"Wow, he was really one of the greats?"

"But of course, all of you are. You are one of the greats too! You just may not know it yet, but I do. I haven't seen you for a while. Are you okay?"

"I'm okay, just busy. Have you seen Jen? I'm meeting her tonight."

"I'm sure she's here somewhere. Feel free to look around. I am going to stay here with the others."

"Okay. I'm sorry, Gina, for your loss."

"Don't be sorry, dear. We are stronger for having his presence here. See you later."

I head toward the dining room thinking Jen may be there, and when she isn't, I go ahead and order a coke and sit at a comfy couch table. I am halfway through my drink when Jen casually walks in and sees me. Our server appears back at the table to take her drink order too.

"What do you want to eat, Jen? I'm in the mood for a cheeseburger."

"I could go for that. Let's order when he comes back." And right on cue, refills arrive, and food orders are placed.

"So, Eve, spill it, what's going on?"

"Well, first off, how are you?"

"I'm good. Enjoying work and enjoying my daughter. After everything that happened my mom is still fabulous. Honestly, I'm dying to hear what's going on with you."

"Where do I start? My sister Hope is getting married in a few months then moving away to London with her husband."

"Really? How do you feel about that?"

"She's my big sister, so of course, I'm happy for her. But, she's quitting school and I don't think that's a good idea."

"Why not?"

"You know how I feel. What if her husband leaves her one day and she's left on her own without an education to fall back on?"

"Do you really think that would happen?"

"Does anybody really know what can happen in the future?"

"True, but you have to think positive and stay supportive."

"I know. I will have to. She is over the moon."

"I can imagine. So what about you Eve? What's going on with you?"

"Well, I'm asking Ben to come home for the wedding."

"You are! That's huge? So, your parents haven't met him yet?"

"No, I've talked about him a bit."

"Things are good with Ben?"

"Yes. Actually, I wanted to tell you, I was proud of your talking to Melinda."

"Thanks. It wasn't easy."

"So, she told you everything?" I ask.

"You knew?" Jen looked shocked. "You didn't say

anything."

"I got an overview from Gina and have been trying to piece everything together. I didn't want to tell you anything until I knew for sure."

"Well, if you figured it involves her, Kerrington Prep, and that asshole Eric then you know it all."

"How crazy is that, Jen, like really?"

"It's awful. I honestly feel worse for her than I do for myself."

"Obviously, a tiger can't change its stripes."

By now, our food has arrived at the table and we are half eating, half nodding while chewing our burgers and fries.

"Eve, what time is it?"

"I don't think it matters here."

"True. What time is it at home?"

"My watch says 6:55pm, eastern standard time, of course. That's what time I got here."

"Gosh, I always forget that time literally stops when we're here."

"I know. I kind of like it," I say with a grin.

"It's still weird to me, I must admit."

"Speaking of, I should head home. Let's plan another date soon.

"Deal!" We hug and kiss good-bye and both head back to our own lives.

My World: Chapter Nineteen

At home, one day seems to run into the next one during the summer break. Each week includes errands with Mom and Hope, breakfast catch up times with Dad, and phone calls and texts with Ben. (He agreed to be my date for my sister's wedding this fall.) Needless to say, the two and half months fly by before I'm back at Kerrington Prep for my second year. I'm only there a few weeks before the fall wedding weekend arrives.

Back home, my maid-of-honor dress is delivered, so Mom takes me to the bridal shop to get alterations. I know I will be entertaining cousins, aunts, uncles, and extended family in a few days. I call Ben when I get back home.

"Hey Ben, when are you coming to Virginia?"

"Sooner than you think. In three days from now, I will be at your airport. Will you be picking me up?"

"Of course. My dad and I will be there. Keep me posted on your ETA."

"You got it! Enjoy the time with your family. Talk

me up."

"I won't need to talk you up, but I will. See you soon."

I run downstairs to find Dad on the couch and say, "Dad, we're picking up Ben from the airport in three days."

"Just tell me when. I'm excited to meet him."

"I'm excited for you to meet him too." I pause then I add, "Do we really like Sam, Dad?"

"Yes, your mother and I do."

"But what about Hope just up and quitting school and moving?"

"When you get married, you often have to make sacrifices."

"But her education?"

"There are schools in London, Eve, she can finish up her courses and graduate there. She just can't sit at home all day while Sam is working."

"I guess that's true, but how are we going to visit her?"

"Just like we visit you."

"You guys never come up to school."

"That's not true. We came to move you in."

"Mom came.

"We came for your birthday and parents' weekend."

"That's true."

"What did I do to make both of my daughters want to move so far away?"

"Or what did you do right?"

"Nice try."

Mom and Hope come running in the door with bags hanging off every limb.

"We're back. What's for dinner?"

Dad responds, "I didn't how long you would be. How about pancakes for dinner?"

Hope cheers, "Yes, Dad's pancakes are the best!"

Soon, Dad flips the pancakes off the skillet and onto each of our plates. I get my plate first and go to sit down and start eating. I still have not found a restaurant pancake that is half as good as my Dad's. Mom has a plate full of pancakes and bacon and a glass of orange juice in her hand. We sit around the table enjoying breakfast for dinner.

"Is Ben still coming to the wedding?" Mom asked once we are comfortable and have started eating. "I know you were going to call him to see."

"Yes, he's coming in a few days. Dad and I are picking him up from the airport."

"Can't wait to meet him," Hope shrieks with delight.

"I'm looking forward to meeting Ben, too," Mom starts. "Isn't he a student at Kerrington too?"

"He actually is an upper classman at the public school right near campus."

"Wasn't the other young man a student at Kerrington?"

"Matt," I replied curtly.

"Do you ever talk to him?" Mom inquires.

"Not since he left and went to London."

"I guess everything happens in London," Hope interjects.

"I see." Mom continues eating and doesn't press the issue further. I don't recall the exact details I shared with my parents, but I'm pretty sure they are not too keen on my social life. They like to remind me they sent me to the best schools to get in the best universities to get the best jobs.

When I decide not to offer up details, Mom goes back to talking to Hope about her wedding. She's on cloud nine to plan such a "spectacular event" as she repeatedly says. Mom always loved telling us about my great aunt Sophia who was proposed to in her early twenties and didn't accept. After that, she apparently lived her life saying, "If I knew that was the only proposal I was ever going to receive, I would have said yes." Mom always said it amusingly, but I secretly pray that it doesn't happen to me too. You know those family curses that skip a generation. Hope is officially in the clear.

She is in her own world and does not actually sense the tension between mom and me. Then Mom speaks again.

"Eve, this is the first real boyfriend you have. Matt doesn't count because we never met him. Is there anything else we should know about him?"

"He's from Boston, his father is a lawyer, and he's black."

"That's great," Dad responds. I know Dad and Hope are cool with whatever. Mom is more into what other people will think.

"Just didn't want you to be surprised."

"Okay," Dad says. Mom says nothing.

"Will he be the only black man at the wedding?" I ask in the moment.

"Don't be silly," Mom finally chimes in, "Your dad's good friends, the Washingtons, will be there."

"And some of Sam's best friends are hot British black men. They're all coming to the states just for the wedding."

Eager to change the subject, I say, "Speaking of-are you ready? What's on tap for tomorrow?"

Mom answers, "We have one more fitting for the both of you and a final trip to the reception site. The shower and rehearsal dinner are the following day. Then, Saturday is the big day!"

Hope sits beaming while Mom rattles off the itinerary.

I turn to Dad, "We will pick up Ben after the shower. He's coming to the rehearsal."

"And I've already set up the guest bedroom for him," Mom replies quickly. She's quiet a moment before she adds, "Let's leave here by 11:30 and head over to the dress shop."

"Sounds good," said Hope.

We clear the table before I take a shower and retreat to my room for the night. I have a feeling this will be the end of my quiet time for a few days, so I relish in it.

Chapter Twenty

The next morning, I'm the last one down for breakfast, so I grab a biscuit and piece of watermelon while leaning over the counter. Hope already looks the part of the blushing bride standing in the kitchen wearing white jeans and a flowy ivory top. Mom tells me to finish eating and meet her in the car. Hope sits up front. Sunglasses on, I jump in the back, wearing a basic black top and blue jeans.

"You girls look just beautiful," Mom says, ever the optimist as she falls into the driver's seat.

"Do you like the bridesmaid dress, Eve? It really fit the other girls perfectly," Hope questions.

"Yes, I liked it; I hope mine fits this time though. We had to make some alterations."

"I'm sure it will; I'm worried about my own dress."

"Why? You look great."

"The pancakes and bacon last night didn't help. Remind me not to eat three meals a day until Saturday." I roll my eyes hearing this comment from my one hundred ten-pound sister.

"That's going to be hard when every event planned involves food," I respond.

"I know. Can't we all enjoy a liquid diet?"

"What's that?" Mom asks.

"Never mind," Hope says.

The seamstress in the dress shop greets us at the door, ready for our appointment; she assigns her co-worker to me while she caters to my sister, the bride-to-be. I end up dressing myself but step out for the assistant to zip me up.

"Perfect!" Mom raves."

"Thank goodness," I respond, relieved. "I didn't get the shoes yet because I didn't know the length of the dress."

"That's no problem," the salesclerk answers, "We have shoes here for you to choose from."

"Nice, one stop shopping, I like it."

"I'll bring some pairs to you for you to try on."

"Thank you." I stand beside my mom listening to Hope behind the dressing curtain getting emotional.

"Are you okay, Hope?" I whisper into the curtain.

"Yes, I'm okay. Here I come."

The seamstress opens the curtain and there stands Hope, an absolute vision in white with the perfect little tears streaming down her cheeks."

"You must not cry like this on the big day, Hope, your

makeup will smear." I try to lighten the moment.

"I won't. Do you like it, Eve?"

"I love it, and Sam will too."

"Do you think so?" she asks hesitantly.

"I know so. Why are you crying?"

"It's just a huge change."

"Hope, if you're not ready, you don't have to do this." As I speak, I watch the faces of my mother and the shop owners turn into distress.

"No, I want to get married. I'm ready."

"Alright then, let's wrap up the dresses," Mom exclaims not wanting to participate in such a serious conversation.

"Where's yours, Mom?" I asked. "You are the mother of the bride."

Hope answers for her. "Oh, Mom is rocking a pastel pant suit she bought a few months ago. It's already in her closet at home."

"Get it. Mom!" I shout.

"You girls are too funny. I want to be comfortable, and it is. Let's drop these dresses home then grab a bite to eat."

"Mom, I just said no to meals. I'm still full from last night and the muffin this morning."

"Fine then. Eve, would you like to go out to lunch, just you and me?"

"Yea, let's do that."

"Great, we'll drop your sister home with the dresses. You pick where you want to go."

"Felipe's; I really would love some fish tacos."

"Felipe's it is."

We pull into the restaurant lot a few minutes before the lunch crowd is due to show up. Mom sees a table of ladies she knows as soon as we walk in, so I get the table. I am hardly situated in the booth when the server walks over to me.

"Hi, welcome to Felipe's, what can I get you to drink?"

That's when I glance up from the table.

"Rachel? Is that you?"

I can't believe she's standing in front of me and has aged so much in a year.

"Eve, how are you doing? You look great!"

"Thank you. I'm doing well. How about you?"

"I'm all right, new job."

"Right, right, which school are you going to?"

"I'm at the public school right around the corner so I walk to work. I didn't go away like you did. I wanted to be closer to my mom and everybody."

"That's great." *That was such a lie.* I couldn't remember the exact rules of the alternate world. Can you talk to someone about it that was in it before? Do you cut off communication with someone who is kicked out of the alternate world? Do they have any memory of the alternate world once they are removed? I may need some clarification on these rules. Just then my mom walks over to the table.

"Mom, you remember Rachel, right?"

"Well, hi there, it's been a while."

"Yes, ma'am, how are you?"

"I'm great. I'd like an iced tea please."

"Sure. And you, Eve?"

"Water's good for me."

"Okay, I'll be back shortly to take your order."

"Oh my gosh, Mom, that was so rude."

"What?" She actually looks oblivious.

"Did you see her? She looks so different."

"I never guessed you two are the same age. She looks so much older than you. I wonder how long she has been working here. It seems difficult for her to focus."

"I heard she had some tough times."

"Oh, who did you hear that from?"

"I can't remember." *Lie.* I look down to examine my menu even though I came here simply for Mahi Mahi fish tacos.

Rachel immediately returns with our drinks and takes our order for lunch. When she collects our menus, I request chips and salsa to start.

"Oh sorry, I forgot about that," she mutters.

"No problem," I respond.

"See what I mean?" Mom whispers when Rachel is out of ear shot.

"Mom!" I discipline. She brushes off my scolding and changes the subject.

"I trust you have an outfit for the rest of the events?

"Yes, I do. This week shopping was perfect."

"And you went shopping for the gifts too?"

"Gift cards."

"Great idea."

"Well, she returns everything people buy her anyway, so this is the easiest."

"True."

"Who were those ladies over there?"

"Oh, they go to the same Mass as we do, and they're so excited about Hope's wedding."

"Are they invited?"

"No, they are just excited."

"Or nosy," I add.

Mom doesn't pay any mind to my comment and begins to tell me about their own children's weddings, how Hope's compares to theirs, and blah, blah blah. She is still talking when the lunch arrives steaming hot. I savor every bite of my tacos while Mom carries on, occasionally stopping to eat the potato chips on her plate.

"Is everything good here?" Rachel stops in to ask.

"Yes, thank you," Mom states.

"So, what are you in town for anyway, Eve?"

"Oh, my sister Hope is getting married."

"Oh, I didn't know that. When is it?"

"This Saturday."

"Oh wow. That's cool." She lingers a bit then says, "Let me know if you need anything else." She smiles and returns to the kitchen.

"Has she always been like that?" Mom asks.

"Like what?"

"She's a little spacey and a bit delayed in response."

"I think it's the drugs."

"What?" Mom shrieks.

"Nothing." *I've got to text Erin.*

Mom and I wrap up our lunch and ask for the check.

"Is there anything else you'd like to do this afternoon?" Mom asks.

"I'm good."

"Alright then, let's get on home and check on your sister."

As we're walking out, Rachel comes over to say bye one more time. She hangs by the door, watching us leave and get into the car. *Now, I wonder if she knows I was in the alternate world when she was still there.*

Chapter Twenty-One

Once in the house, I run upstairs and jump on my bed like old times to text Erin the information.

Eve: Hey girl!

Erin: Hey, what's up?

Eve: It's Hope's wedding weekend.

Erin: Yes, how's it going?

Eve: It's busy, but I had to text you. What are you doing today?

Erin: No definite plans, why?

Eve: Wanna meet?

Erin: Can you get away?

Eve: Please, I'll be in wedding festivities for the next two days. It's fine.

Erin: Alright, when do you want to meet?

Eve: Thirty Minutes. The coffee shop. Will that work?

Erin: That's good. See you then.

Eve: Great, bye!

"Dad," I yell running down the stairs, "I'm heading out for a bit."

"Where are you headed?" he replies.

"Going to meet Erin."

"Okay."

Mom hears the conversation and comes into the kitchen.

"Where are you going, Eve?"

"Erin wants to meet for coffee."

"Will you be back for dinner?"

"Yes, I will only be gone for like an hour."

I walk a few blocks over into the café to see the back of Erin talking to a really cute guy I've never seen before. She must have told him she was meeting a friend here because I see him kind of perk up and smile like he's signaling me over. Erin must have noticed too because she turns around to smile and motion me over. I walk toward the table, and Erin is up on her feet to greet with me a big hug.

"Hey, Eve! You look great!" Erin cheerily says. Then, the guy with her stands up.

"Eve, this is my boyfriend, Sean."

"Hi, it's nice to meet you," Sean says while shaking my hand, "Erin has told me so much about you."

"Nice to meet you too," I respond.

"I know you two have a lot to talk about, so I'm going to head out." Sean leans down to give Erin a kiss on the cheek before he leaves.

"Thanks Sean. I'll call you later," Erin says before turning her attention to me.

"Sit, girl, sit!

"So, who is Sean and when did you get a boyfriend? I thought I was supposed to be on the lookout for you."

"I met Sean about a month ago. He's a member of the country club where I'm a host this summer."

"So, he's rich?" I ask, intrigued.

"I haven't asked, but I get the feeling he is. He goes to St. Stephen's.

"And you met him at the club?" I ask.

"Yes, I went in one night to pick up my paycheck and he was just sitting by himself."

"So, you all just started talking?"

"He came over to me to ask the time."

"You're kidding!"

"I know. Of all things, really. We all have I-phones in our back pocket, but he was nervous and really sweet. We've been hanging out ever since."

"Do you only hang out here?"

"For now."

"I'm jealous of you," I say very matter of fact.

She laughs and asks why.

"You don't have any secrets."

"I doubt that seriously," Erin replies laughing again.

My mind drifts off a moment to the biggest secret between

Erin and me and that I can't share with Ben. Sometimes I wonder if that will ultimately affect our relationship.

"You seem happy."

"We are, but I don't know what will happen, you know. We're from two different worlds."

"What?" I'm puzzled.

"You know-he's country club and private school. I'm public school and neighborhood pool."

"That doesn't mean it can't work out. You guys will stay together and learn everything about each other. You will always be a part of your world while experiencing a new world."

"You make it sound so easy."

I realize then I should be taking my own advice.

"For the record, I think you and Ben together is a no brainer."

"Thanks, Erin."

"No problem, now I know this is not the reason you wanted to meet me in person. What's going on?"

"Yes, thank you for keeping me on track. You will never guess who I ran into today."

"Tell me."

"Rachel. She's a waitress at Felipe's. Do you ever go there?"

"No, not in years. Did you talk to her?"

"I did, but she doesn't say much. She didn't look the same either."

“Really?”

“Yes, she seemed almost sluggish.”

“Do you think it was the drugs?”

“You heard that too?”

“Everyone heard that.”

“I’m not sure, but maybe.”

“Wow,” is all Erin can say.”

“Have you seen Ellie at all by chance?”

“I have not. I don’t know if she’s even home this summer.”

That’s who I need to talk to. And I have plenty of time before dinner.

“Interesting. So glad I got to meet Sean. I have to get back home.”

“Good luck with wedding weekend.”

“Thanks, girl. Talk to you soon.”

“Bye.”

ALTERNATE WORLD

There is no GPS available for the alternate world even though Siri thinks she knows everything, so I head straight down Turtle Lane. I walk through two lights then notice a curvy dirt road on the left that I've never seen before. Granted, a lot of new real estate has taken place since I moved away, but this road came out of nowhere. I follow it into a forest of trees and after about a mile come upon the mansion I've seen a hundred times before. *Weird.*

It has never occurred to me how Ellie or Jen or even that great deceased man from London get here themselves. I know there's no time in the alternate world, but there is also no set location. I'm starting to wonder if there's even an urban myth about the alternate world or is it truly only known to its members. How do we know that people like Rachel who have been removed haven't told people about it? She was the one who first mentioned it to me before I had the slightest idea what she was talking about.

I head up the stairs and am greeted by Gina.

"Eve, how goes the wedding weekend?"

"Did I tell you about that, Gina?"

"You don't have to tell me Eve, I know."

"You do?"

"Dear, must I remind you I know all that goes on in the alternate world?"

"But my sister isn't in the alternate world."

"No, but you are, and remember everything on earth is connected to our world, where is where you ultimately live."

"Am I ever going to get a handle on this?"

"When you commit and fully believe," Gina states.

I sigh as I let that sink in. "Well, I'm looking for Ellie. Is she here today?"

"Ahh, yes, she's in the drawing room."

I haven't really spoken to Ellie in a while and certainly not at length in here, so I cautiously walk over to say hello. She smiles as soon as she sees me and tells me I look great. I ask her about Justin, and she lets me know he's on the way.

"That's soo cool that your relationship transcends in both worlds!" I exclaim.

"It is special. I actually want to bring him back home so we can explore our relationship there too."

"Speaking of home. My sister Hope is getting married this weekend."

"That's exciting," she cheeringly says.

"It is. I actually came here to look for you since you're the only person from high school I can talk to about this."

"Okay, what's up?"

"I saw Rachel today. She's a server at Felipe's. Do you talk to her?"

"No, not since seventh grade. Did you all talk today?"

"Yes, but she didn't say much. She didn't look the same either."

"Did you know she was a part of the alternate world?"

"I saw her photo once on the wall, but I never saw her here. Now that I think about it, I haven't seen the photo in a while."

I interject, "Actually, she's not here anymore."

"Why not?"

"Apparently, she got into drugs."

"You're kidding."

"No, and there's something else." I lower my voice to just above a whisper.

"What?" She instinctively whispers back.

"I saw something."

"Where?"

"Here. I can't remember how long ago it was, but I swear it was Rachel."

"What was Rachel?" she asks inquisitively.

"I was here one night trying to get a sense about myself and everyone else who resided here past and present.

I was wandering around the house to gain any insight I could from documents, portraits, you name it. Walking down the main hall, I saw a dim light from a room I'd never noticed before. I followed up the steps to where the door was cracked and peeked in. The lights were off in the room, but there was a circle of at least twelve men sitting on the carpet all holding candles. There was a girl in the center of the circle. I think it was Rachel."

"How do you know? And how come I don't know about this room?"

"All I could hear were low voices of the men, but a flash of pink walked by the crack in the door about every forty-five seconds, so I think Gina was there too, which would explain why I couldn't find her anywhere that particular evening."

"And what were they doing? What was happening?" Ellie is astonished.

"I'm not exactly sure. I heard low, deep voices and a girl crying. It wasn't like she was hurt. It was more like the people were coaxing her or something."

"What do you think it was about?"

"Gina told me when Rachel started doing drugs, they did everything they could to help her here. I think they were having an intervention. It was just creepy."

"Have you asked Gina about it?"

"No, and I'm not going to. I wasn't supposed to see anything. Obviously, they tried to help her in some capacity, and she didn't want to be helped. Believe me, after seeing her in the restaurant, it's evident that she refused the aid.

"So, what can we do?"

"That's just it-Rachel can't talk to us. I'm afraid to ask Gina, so I'm telling you."

"I think we should ask her. Is she here?"

"She greeted me at the door and told me you were in here."

"Alright then, let's go." We pace down the long corridor to the kitchen.

"Gina?" Ellie calls.

"I'm in here," Gina shouts from inside the pantry.

"Gina, do you have a minute? Eve and I wanted to ask you something."

"Sure. What can I do for you?"

"I don't know how to say this, and I'm sorry if I'm out of line," I state.

"You can ask me anything, Eve. This is a no judgment zone."

"I went to lunch today back home and ran into Rachel."

"Oh? How is she?" She seems concerned.

"Not good."

"That's too bad," Gina responds, "She had such potential."

"That's what I wanted to ask you. Do you all offer

therapy here?"

"Therapy?"

"Yes, I remember you previously said something about how you were trying to help Rachel."

"Oh yes, we did."

"How?" Ellie asks.

"Anyway possible. Why do you ask?"

I pipe in, "It's just that I was here one night wandering around, and I think I came upon a private meeting in an upstairs room I've never seen before."

"You mean the intervention space?"

"I guess so. I don't know."

"If one of our own is in such a danger on earth, we host an intervention. I call in twelve of our very best members, all with expertise in support and psychology, to assist our member in question. Thankfully, we don't have to do it very often because it is extremely emotionally draining scenario. Unfortunately, this time it didn't work for Rachel. Remember, the alternate world cannot be used as an escape, which is what she wanted to stay here for."

I continue, "Does Rachel remember any of this?"

"I would assume so," Gina says.

"But she's no longer connected with this world, correct?"

"No, she's not. Did she say anything to you?"

"No, and I didn't know if we were allowed to ask her anything."

"About what exactly?"

"About her life in this world."

"Unfortunately, girls, since you didn't connect while you were in here, it wouldn't make a difference if you said anything. To Rachel, everything is now a distant memory if she even remembers anything. She no longer believes this world exists because she's no longer a member. Sadly, if she's still in the same condition as she was before, she probably doesn't know what to think about it anymore."

"I was just wondering," I respond, "And you're right, Gina, she was not in a good place today."

"I'm sorry to hear that, but you ladies are right to inquire about her. I know it comes from a good place-concern for a childhood friend. I am here for you for whatever you may need. We look out for each other here, and we know each other's true selves."

"Thanks Gina," I say, and Ellie concurs.

"I should probably get home. I promised my mom I'd be home for dinner."

Ellie and Gina both go in for a hug before I turn and walk back home. Dad is setting the table when I walk in.

"Hey, kiddo, would you help me make some drinks? We're having spaghetti for dinner."

"Yum. Will do."

"Great, we'll start and save a plate for your mom and Hope. They had to drop off some food for the shower tomorrow."

"Sounds good."

We sit down to say the blessing then twirl our forks around the noodles. After dinner, I call Ben to tell him I'll see him tomorrow and fall asleep dreaming about the moment.

My World:
Chapter Twenty-Two

When my alarm sounds, I know it's the signal for Hope's wedding weekend to officially begin. The morning starts with her bridal shower at Mom's friend Sandy's house. Hope is dressed in white pants and a pink and green top (her wedding colors) and beaming from ear to ear. She is not the least bit shy when she is asked to sit on a huge armchair and open presents with all eyes on her. She is at ease eating chicken salad, fruit salad, and spinach salad while conversing with all of the ladies. She is not uncomfortable at all when people toast her and her new future. Nobody leaves until they each have a turn hugging the bride-to-be and telling her they can't wait to see her tomorrow. I'm so glad that Hope is the one getting married first. I don't think I could handle all this. Thank goodness Dad picks me up a tad early from the event to head to the airport. We are in charge of getting Ben back to Mom and Dad's house and changed before rehearsal today.

How lucky are we that the flight from Boston lands

ten minutes early. Dad parks in the short-term lot and I walk into the airport. While I am not prepared with flowers or a welcome poster, I'm still standing in the right place for Ben to see me as soon as he gets off the plane. He walks into the main breezeway and sees me right away. Perhaps it's because I'm the most overdressed in the common meeting area still wearing my yellow dress. Ben greets me with a huge hug and brief kiss.

"What? No poster for me?" he says laughing.

"Welcome to the South," I respond.

"I like it so far."

"Maybe you should wait a few days before you make that decision."

"Okay."

"Do you have luggage?"

"Yes, I had to check it because my dress bag was my carry on."

"No problem. We'll head downstairs to baggage claim; my dad is parked and waiting right outside there."

"And where's our first stop?"

"Did you eat?"

"Yes."

"Then, our first stop is my home. Hope and Mom should be back from the shower by now. We can have a snack of some sort before rehearsal at the church."

"Sounds great."

Dad sees me coming so he pops the trunk for us to

put Ben's luggage in there then get in the back seat. Dad welcomes Ben to Virginia, and he politely expresses his gratitude for inviting him here. (*So far, so good*, I think.) No one is on the interstate on the way home, so we are back at the house in less than thirty minutes. We pull in the driveway, and Ben hops out to open the trunk of the car and unzip his luggage. By the time I turn around I see him holding a gift bag of New England treats.

"Where did that come from?" I inquire, surprised.

"Another reason I checked my luggage," he smirks.

I walk up the front steps behind Dad, and he follows me right in the front door like he has been here so many times before.

"We're here!" I call, walking in.

"We're in the kitchen," Mom answers.

Sure enough, Mom and Dad are already snacking while Hope is retelling every detail from today's shower that literally ended just an hour earlier.

"Everybody, this is Ben."

Mom stands up to hug him, Dad officially shakes his hand, and Hope waves from her seat at the table.

"This is for you, Mrs. Thompson," Ben says as he presents the basket to my mom.

"Well, thank you, Ben, that is so sweet." Her eyes are smiling when she places the present on the counter.

"Can we get you two something to eat?" Dad asks.

"Yes, you should definitely eat something to tide you

over. Go ahead and give them those mini sandwiches, honey," Mom tells Dad.

Ben and I sit beside Hope, who is snacking on a fruit cup.

"Congratulations, Hope, and thank you for including me on your special day," Ben says.

"I'm so glad you could come. The fact that my sister would even consider bringing you as a "plus one" certainly says something."

I feel my cheeks and chest getting red, so I try to play it off by smiling and taking little bites from my sandwich. Hope must have noticed because she was the first to speak.

"Eve, what color is your dress for rehearsal?" Hope asks.

"I bought a blue and white striped dress back home. Did I show it to you?"

"No, but that sounds perfect."

"Don't worry. I'm not wearing white."

"I know you wouldn't, Eve, but you wouldn't believe the lack of etiquette people have today. My friend Shelley's mother-in-law wore a white pant suit to her own son's wedding."

"Even I know that's not right," Ben chimed in.

"Well, Ben, we definitely want to spend some time with you and get to know you better, but we are very glad you will be spending this special weekend with us," my mom says.

"I am very glad to be here. Thank you very much; I just don't want to be in the way."

"You won't be," I say, "Mom will put you to work if you are."

Everyone laughs at the table except Mom, who simply shakes her head and says, "That's not true."

Dad raises his eyebrows.

"It might be kind of true," he adds.

"I'm going to go shower and then call Sam," Hope announces.

"Sounds good, dear, and don't worry; we'll all be ready on time," Mom says.

"I'm not worried," she shrieks, running up the stairs.

"Well, now that we have a moment to ourselves," Dad starts, "Ben, you're born and raised in Massachusetts, right?"

"Yes, sir, I'm from Boston."

"And did you two meet at school?"

"He's a year ahead of me and goes to a public school nearby," I answer between bites.

"Right. We actually met at a corner coffee shop," Ben clarifies. "I was in the area working with my dad."

"Well, that's so funny," Mom amusingly states.

"Not really, thousands of people are in the coffee shop every day." I respond.

"I actually believe it was just the right place, right time for me," Ben answers.

"Me too," I kiss him on the cheek.

"Do you live on campus?" Dad asks.

"Our house is about 10 minutes from Eve's school."

"That's so nice for your parents. We ask Eve almost every month when she's moving home," Mom says.

"Um, almost every week," I clarify.

"That's because we love you and miss you. Kerrington Prep is another world," Mom adds.

"But we are very proud of our girl," Dad jumps in.

"Do you all ever come up to visit? I'd love to show you around the city on your next trip," Ben says.

"Mom, your turn!" Hope screams from the top of the stairs.

"We will definitely plan a trip for the fall semester," Mom answers while she stands up preparing for the shower. Mom turns to Dad, "Honey, why don't you shower in the hall bathroom, then Eve, you show Ben where the guest bathroom is, and you can shower in our bathroom."

"Sounds good, Mom."

Once the kitchen clears out, I look at Ben and he seems cool as a cucumber.

"You alright? It's only going to get crazier."

"I'm great. I love your family. I really like knowing where you came from."

"Come on, I'll show you to your room."

"We have separate rooms?" he asks in disbelief.

"Welcome to the South." I say, smiling.

Thank goodness everyone in my family cleans up well and fast. We are all ready to go about an hour and a half later. Ben's blue tie perfectly matches the stripes in my dress, and Hope is all lit up.

"Ben, would you take a family picture?" Mom asks as she shoves the camera in his hand. Once she is pleased with the shots, we take two cars to the church for the rehearsal. Mom drives Hope, and Dad drives Ben and me. The church is so close that not much conversation takes place; it's basically Dad pointing out local landmarks, which include the mall, a cemetery, and the middle school Hope and I attended. Can you tell we live in the suburbs?

We walk in the church and are instantly surrounded by some of our family members and the entire wedding party. A few hugs and greetings are exchanged before the wedding planner has us line up to practice. No second is spared from here on out. I am paired with Sam's cousin Mitch, a very mild-mannered Englishman; we exchange a few pleasantries before we are cued to walk down the aisle. We are the final couple before the bride makes her grand entrance. The rehearsal takes a total of about fifteen minutes, a much shorter version of the official Catholic wedding that will occur tomorrow. Everyone looks prepared for the big day as we leave for the rehearsal dinner.

Chapter Twenty-Three

We caravan to the restaurant Hope and Sam chose, a sea-food restaurant in the city. Dad and Ben are in the front seat engaged in conversation about nothing I'm really interested in, so I zone out. My mind goes straight to my alternate world, as I realize at the rehearsal that not one of them is in the world with me. Not Ben. Not my family. I don't understand it. The alternate world represents individuals across the globe that are true to themselves, and no one from my family is there with me besides my great, great grandmother. I just don't get it. I'm really on a mission now to find out why.

Dad's sharp right turn into the parking deck jerks me, and I'm back in my thoughts of reality.

"Are you okay?" Ben asks when he turns to look at me.

"Yes, why?"

"You looked like you were a million miles away."

"No, I think I'm hungry."

"Well, then you're at the right place, Evie," Dad adds.

Sam's family is in charge of the dinner, so our family

really gets to sit back and relax. We are served a four-course meal, which I savor during a slide show presentation about how Hope and Sam met. We also listen to a few speeches from his friends and family; I guess our family's on tomorrow.

Again, I scan the room to see if I recognize anyone from "the other world." I know that I'm not perfect, far from it, so I really don't know why I was chosen among everyone in my family. I'm gathering that most people have a story to tell that they likely choose not to share. I'm really wondering what secrets my parents are keeping from me and maybe even what Ben isn't telling me about himself either.

I try to get out of my thoughts and back into the present moment again where Hope and Sam are now making the rounds to all the tables expressing their gratitude and excitement for sharing the weekend with them. I'm wondering if Hope realizes what journey she is about to embark on. Besides marriage, she is moving overseas with her new husband. And my parents think Boston is far? How often will they be visiting London? And if they do visit my older sister more than they visit me, I'll be ticked.

I take the moment to grab Ben by the hand and introduce him to some of our extended family. I decided to invite him to share this celebration with me, so I definitely want to include him in everything. He charms my grandparents, cousins, aunts, uncles, and family friends. Despite the fact we have not even graduated high school, a few of my aunts ask if we can see ourselves getting married. We both laugh it off because it's another example of what older people deem important. *Maybe that's why none of them are in the alternate world? Who knows?* It is definitely a generational thing. I actually don't recall anyone asking about my summer job or school. Once the room begins to clear out, my family poses for a few more photos before we leave ourselves. This entire room of people will be together again tomorrow.

Mom, Dad, Ben, and I stand to the side while Hope and Sam do their own good-byes (hugs, kisses, you name it). They must part tonight and won't be reunited until tomorrow at 2pm when she walks down the aisle to her groom. Mom drives Hope home so Dad takes Ben and me in his car. Once we get home, everyone has the same idea, which is just to change into comfy clothes. Dad, Hope, and Ben reconvene in the den, so I take the opportunity to pull Mom into the kitchen for which I hope will be a heart-to-heart. We never do this, so I'm not sure what it will look like. Mom makes us both a cup of hot tea and we sit across from each other at the round kitchen table.

"Are you tired yet, Eve?" Mom asks.

"I'm good. It will hit me at the end of the weekend. You?" I respond.

"I'm not the one who worked summer camp the last three weeks, then flew home."

"True, but I'm okay. What do you think about Ben?"

"He definitely seems more polite and handsome than everything I heard about Matt."

"I agree. He's amazing. But Mom, how do know if he's the one? Like, I know it sounds crazy, but I can actually picture us together forever, but with you and Dad, how did you know?"

"You don't sound crazy. Plenty of people marry their high school sweethearts. I know it's corny too, honey, but you just know. Can you picture a day without Ben? If not, then that's when you know."

"Do you ever feel like you and Dad live in two different worlds?"

"Of course I do. Your dad is a dreamer; his head is always in the clouds."

"That's not what I really mean."

"I know what you mean, and I believe it's better **not** to be exactly the same as your significant other. You can learn more about yourself when you're with someone who is different from you. Hope and Sam are not alike; they simply complement each other."

"That makes sense. So you and Daddy were always opposite?"

"Oh yes. That's why you and Hope differ in some ways; you're more like your dad and Hope is a little me at times. What's really on your mind?"

I can't even begin to tell my own mother about a new life I'm leading, so I just start talking about my relationship with Ben, since that's what she thinks the issue is anyway.

"I think that Ben and I complement each other, but I know we are not exactly the same. We have pretty different pasts."

"Everybody has a past, but obviously your differences brought you to the same place."

"That's true."

"What's really worrying you, Eve?"

"I'm just confused. Hope is ready to take the plunge with Sam. You and Dad have been together forever. I know it didn't feel right with Matt, and I do love Ben. I guess I just want to hear my future is right with Ben."

"Honey, no one knows what the future holds. And at your age, you have your whole life ahead of you."

"I know, but I would love a little clue, you know? I don't want to make any wrong decisions." I start getting a little teary eyed, which Mom also notices, which changes her tune a little bit.

"You know, honey, Daddy and I went through some tough times ourselves before you were born."

"I didn't know that."

"Well, it's not something you like to share with your children."

"What happened?"

"We were in North Carolina dating when he finally proposed. I said yes right before he told me he had taken a job in Maryland. This came out of left field for me since I thought we were going to live our lives and raise our children in North Carolina, in the south."

"Mom, we live in Virginia."

"Richmond, Virginia is Mid-Atlantic."

"Okay," I mutter and continue to listen.

"Your father basically told me he loved me but loved his work too. He didn't understand how important our life in the Carolinas was to me. I wasn't giving in. He wasn't giving in. So, I told him we couldn't get married if we couldn't agree on where to live."

"I can't believe this, Mom. Were you apart for long?"

"About three months, but it felt like forever. I returned his ring and said that I needed some time to think. I felt like he had put his work ahead of me, and I didn't want to be second in anyone's life.

"No way!" My chin drops.

"Your father did not like that all. My phone rang at least three times a week over the course of about three months. Your grandmother finally sat me down and talked about how the purpose of marriage is to compromise; your dad and I are both pretty stubborn. One day when he called, my tone had changed and I told him I'd like to meet with him, which he agreed to with the ring in hand. That's the first thing I noticed."

"Aww, Dad, always the optimist."

"He is. I told him I loved him and was willing to compromise. He told me he had made some calls and found out he could work in Washington DC."

"We decided we could both pick up and move to Richmond, Virginia, together, and he would commute. I could essentially find a teaching job anywhere. We never talked about it again and thus here we are today."

"Wow, Mom! That was huge."

"It felt huge at the time, but honestly, once we decided to compromise and do the best thing for everyone involved, that's when things work out. That's love. That's what Hope has with Sam, and that's what I wish for you when the time is right."

"Thanks for telling me that, Mom."

"I just want you to be happy, enjoy your childhood, and don't waste any time worrying or stressing yourself out. What's meant to be will be."

"Thanks, Mom. I love you."

"Love you, baby, and I love Ben too, from the little I know about him."

"Thanks. I should probably go check on him. I've left him long enough with Dad and Hope."

Mom and I walk into the living room to discover that Hope is already upstairs. Dad said once she went up, she never came back down. He and Ben look so comfortable watching television. Ben is sitting in the lounge chair, so

I walk up and put my hands on his shoulders.

"How's it going in here?" I ask him.

"Fine. Your dad and I seem to have the same taste in TV."

"Well, that's good. Are you tired?"

"Yes, Ben," Mom chimes in, "Please don't feel like you have to keep my husband company. You've had a long day of travel."

"I'm headed up to shower and go to bed myself, if you're ready."

"That's perfect. Goodnight, Mr. and Mrs. Thompson. Thank you for welcoming me into your family this weekend."

"Goodnight, Ben. We're glad you're here. Get some sleep for the big day."

I lead Bed upstairs and tell him to shower first while I sneak into Hope's room."

I knock at the same time I let myself in, and she is still up. She's perfectly perched against her pillow scrolling through photos from earlier today."

"Hey, girl!" she greets me and looks so happy.

"Are you ready for tomorrow?"

"Ready as I'll ever be."

"I'll be right beside you the whole time, Hope. I love you."

"I love you, too, Eve. And I will stand beside you if you decide to marry Ben."

"Real funny." I reply. I give her a look, which she knows very well.

She just sheepishly smiles and says, "I like him."

"Good night, sleep tight," I whisper while closing her door.

Ben walks out of the bathroom in a towel the same time I am exiting Hope's room, and yes, he looks good. I am instantly drawn to his wet body and give him a quick kiss before saying good night and sending him to the guest room. My parents are still downstairs. I shower myself before climbing into my childhood bed. I know I must go right to sleep since I need to be rested for tomorrow. After talking to Mom, I realize that I am lucky where I am right now, both in this world and the alternate world. Things happen as they should and are out of my control. I fall fast asleep.

Chapter Twenty-Four

I hear Hope and Mom up and at 'em earlier than expected in the morning. I stay in bed until Mom peeks in and says it's time for me to get up. I join Mom and Hope down in the kitchen in casualwear since the three of us have a special appointment with the hair and make-up stylist. Ben comes down to the kitchen just as we are leaving. I tell him the details of the morning and tell him to enjoy a boy's day with my dad.

At the salon, all eyes are on Hope (as it should be) as she talks about how she envisions the rest of the day to go. While we are getting our hair done, Mom shares stories from recent weddings she has attended and boldly states how she knows that Hope's wedding will be by far the most beautiful.

After two hours, we are "picture perfect". We drive home so Dad can chauffeur us to St. Matthew's before he returns home to get ready. He will bring Ben later when all of the groomsmen are due to arrive. The wedding director greets us at the entrance and shuffles us into a room where the other bridesmaids will meet us. We enjoy snacks (cheese, crackers, grapes, and champagne) while we all get dressed. Mom and I get dressed while Hope's bridesmaids arrive one by one, dress in hand. Everyone looks beautiful; we all take turns popping grapes in our mouths and complimenting each other. Pretty soon the photographer arrives to document Hope getting ready with before the procession begins.

As Mom predicted, the wedding is beautiful, and I have the best position beside my sister at the altar. My dad and Sam both get tears in their eyes when they see Hope walking down the aisle; Hope remains the strong one. Even my mom, front row, and center, has a tissue to her eyes. The music, the readings, the flowers, and the entire ceremony are all so perfect. I glance at the guests throughout the service and always catch Ben smiling and looking directly at me.

The reception is just as gorgeous and full of excitement. Since everyone worth talking to was at the dinner last night, I really get to enjoy the night with Ben and my family. He stands beside me during the speeches, cheers me on during the one I give, and dances with me the whole time. It is true that the magic of a wedding really makes you think of your own happiness and future. And while we don't know what the future entails, I do know I'm full of joy in this moment for my sister, for my parents, and for my Ben. As always, no one wants to leave a Thompson party; Hope's wedding is no exception. The DJ helps out when he announces the last dance.

Ben and I are already on the dance floor and just get closer for our final dance together.

"You look beautiful," Ben says to me as he turns me around.

"You look pretty good yourself," I respond.

"Thank you for bringing me here. I know it was a big deal for you to have me around your entire family. It means a lot to me."

"Well, they love you, so it's worked out!"

"Did you think they wouldn't love this?" he flirts, gesturing towards himself.

"True, but you never know with my family."

"Well, I know I already love them almost as much as I love you."

All I can do is smile and rest my head on his broad shoulders. I want to savor these moments with him, especially since I know he flies home tomorrow. We finish the dance intertwined, moving to the beat of the music until the DJ announces it's time to send off the happy couple. We all grab a sparkler from a silver bucket sitting outside of the venue before we line up to shine Hope and Sam down carpet into their town car. Hope doesn't climb into the car until she hugs Mom, Dad, and me. Once the car is out of sight, the guests begin to file out. Dad then drives Mom, Ben, and me home. Mom beams the whole way home, proud of the very first wedding she put on. I know she's already excited to plan another one soon, which by default will be mine, whenever I decide to do so, which is no time soon. Once home, we all individually shower then crash.

Chapter Twenty-Five

My phone dings at 9:30 the next morning, signaling that we have to take Ben to the airport at noon. We have breakfast with Mom and Dad before we have to leave. Dad makes his famous pancakes and scrambled eggs for Ben to have a full stomach before flying home. You never know what food airport terminals have to offer. I keep thinking that on my flight home, I could slip into the alternate world and forego the airtime, but sadly that's not how it works. Like Gina says, the alternate world is not an escape.

"When will you be back to visit us, Ben?" Mom asks.

He looks at me before responding.

"I'd love to come back soon, Mrs. Thompson."

"You certainly are always welcome to come visit us both up North," I continue.

"We just may have to do that," Dad mentions, "Especially since we are planning a London trip to see your sister."

"What? No one told me this."

"We haven't figured out the date yet, Eve," Mom says. "Once we do we were going to tell you. Can you believe the trip to London from DC is practically the same length as it is to the other side of the country?"

"Well, then, you have no excuses not to see us if you can go there. The flight is direct and a little over an hour."

"We will visit both of our daughters," Dad adds while serving our plates.

I smile and dig in. Dad is designated to take Ben to the airport in about forty minutes, and I'm riding with him. We finish breakfast and pack up his luggage. Ben leans in to give my mom a hug before we depart, which I view as sweet.

Dad drives us to the airport terminal to drop Ben off. We all get out of the car, and Dad gives Ben a handshake before he and I enter the double doors. I give him a long hug and tell him that I'll be back at school in less than three weeks.

Wow! Summer break does fly by. Didn't I just get home?

Those three weeks seem to go even faster than the first part of vacation. With the wedding over and Hope gone, it's finally calm and quiet around the house. Mom and Dad cook my favorite meals and treat me to dinner at my favorite spots. Most of my friends are on their own family trips away at the beach before they start back to school. Now that this is my second year at school, my parents buy me a flight back. I'm returning to the same room, which is already decorated and ready to go. The big question is will I be assigned a new roommate. It was nice to have my own space when Jen left, but it's so much fun to have someone with you to go to lunch or dinner or walk around the campus track. I guess I'll find out soon enough.

Chapter Twenty-Six

The day of my own departure arrives, and just like before, Dad makes pancakes and scrambled eggs before taking me to the airport. I hug Mom before getting in the car.

"Come visit soon, Mom."

"I will, honey! We will be there before you know it. I love you, honey."

"Thanks, Mom."

I hop in the shotgun seat with tears welling up in my eyes and am silent for a minute before Dad interrupts my thoughts.

"You ready for your second year, kiddo?"

"I think so. It's a lot easier to return then to begin."

"That's true in everything. I'm so proud of you. You have already grown up so much."

"Thanks, Daddy."

We pull up at the same terminal we left Ben at last month, and Dad gets my luggage out of the trunk and gives me the biggest bear hug before I walk toward the security line. I take several paces forward before turning around and giving one more final wave from a distance (safer than another hug, which will make me breakdown into tears, and I do not cry in public). Once I'm seated at the right gate, I text Ben and let him know my flight is on time and I'll be there around 3. He responds instantly saying he will be waiting for me in the arrival circle.

I get off the plane and walk down the hall to where Ben is standing with a huge smile on his face. Like a gentleman, he carries my bag to his car in the hourly parking deck. On the ride to school, we decide to pick up take out and he asks if he could spend the night with me. Fingers crossed I don't have a roommate there waiting for me. He suggests that we go to my dorm room to move back in and find out but to plan to spend the night at his house. It has been over three weeks since we have had real quality time for just the two of us.

School looked the same minus the fact a brand-new group of students are moving in How funny that only a year ago that was me, unsure and a nervous wreck. This time, I'm confident and at ease. I unlock the door to my room, which has an envelope taped to the front, and I find that no one else has moved in. The envelope includes a welcome back letter and a new roommate notice: Kara Roberts from Birmingham, Alabama will be our newest addition in two days.

"I have a new roommate," I say to Ben.

"That's cool. Are you excited?" he asks.

"I think it will be good. She's from Alabama and just starting, so I'll be able to show her the ropes."

"When does she move in?"

"Two days."

"Well, then I'm going to spend as much time as I can for the next two days until I have to share you with Kara."

"I like the sound of that." I snag the same bag I traveled with and lock the door back. Once back in Ben's car, he drives us directly to our favorite Chinese takeout place while I call and place our order-egg rolls, fried rice with shrimp, and extra fortune cookies. It should be ready in twenty-five minutes.

"Do you have enough clothes packed to stay over at my house?" he giggles.

"Only three months' worth," I reply.

"Good, although, I was kind of thinking you wouldn't need any clothes tonight. My parents are gone again." Ben smiles when he says it.

My flushed cheeks reveal my response.

"Did you enjoy the wedding weekend?" I change the subject.

"I really did. Thank you for inviting me. Do you miss your family?"

"I do, but now that my sister is moving across the pond, it's not exactly the same back home, you know?"

"I do, but I also know how much you love your family."

"And I love it here at school, and I love hanging out with you."

"Well, I'm good with that." After a few more stoplights, we pull into the parking lot of the restaurant, and I'm instantly starving. Ben hands me a credit card with his parents' name on it.

"Use this."

I take it and run inside to grab the food while he keeps the car running; Mr. Wong greets me with a hello and my order. I'm tempted to eat a cookie this instant, but I contain myself since we are almost at his house and I've already waited this long. Instead, I hop into the car with two brown bags in hand. Ben takes a few neighborhood streets home before he parks in the garage. He grabs our luggage while I hold the food. We sashay into his home, and he drops both the duffel bag in the front hallway as we head for the bar stools to eat dinner. We both practically inhale our dinner before I walk straight into his bathroom, throw my clothes on the floor, and hop in the shower.

"You didn't tell me it was going to go like this," I hear Ben say as he opens the steamy shower door. His clothes are off in an instant, and he is in the shower with me. He pushes me against the tile wall while he passionately kisses me on the mouth before slowly moving down to show equal and gentle attention to other parts of my body. The hot water falls on the both of us for a good amount of time until we both decide to turn the knob off. I dry off completely before putting on shorts and a tank top while Ben waltzes around the bedroom in a towel.

"What do you want to do now?" he asks me with a boyish grin.

"I guess I should have asked to use your bathroom. Sorry."

"Believe me. You have nothing to be sorry about, and my parents are at the beach house for the weekend. I told you I have two days to spend with you."

"I didn't know you were serious. Do you have any work to do for your dad?"

"I do, but I'd much rather put my energy elsewhere if you know what I mean?"

"I do."

"Okay, then, I'll pour the wine."

I take a bottle and glasses to the den, and Ben fills them up then puts the bottle back in the fridge. Lounging back on the couch with my feet on the coffee table, Ben walks back in, wearing his athletic shorts and t-shirt. *He looks SOOO good.* Ben sits beside me on the couch and starts kissing my neck. He turns on the television then we take turns displaying multiple signs of affection to the other. After an entire bottle of dessert wine is consumed, I'm feeling a little tipsy and somewhat over tired, but I get up the nerve to say what has been weighing on my mind.

"Ben, I just want you to know there is nowhere else in the world I want to be than with you."

"Forever?" Ben asks as he moves my hair out of my face and tucks it behind my ear."

"That's a lot of pressure," I reply but am secretly over the moon.

"You can handle pressure well from what I've seen."

"That's true."

"I told you before and I'll tell you again. I love you just the way you are, Eve."

"I Love you too. Goodnight, Ben."

"Night."

The peacefulness I feel falling asleep and waking up beside him cannot be described in words alone. It definitely feels more than right, and like Mom said, two people in love don't have to be exactly the same. And honestly, Ben could have secrets of his own. Most people do.

Phones alarms are sounding less than eight hours later. Ben is up and dressed before I even remove myself from my pillow. I try to take at least ten more minutes to rest my eyes until I wake up. I definitely need caffeine and maybe even a chocolate chip muffin. I get up and get dressed in order to treat myself. Ben and I walk around the corner to the coffee shop and smile recalling the first time I met Ben in this very space. While we wait for our order, I text Erin.

Eve: Everybody loved Ben!

Erin: I'm not surprised. He is a catch.

Eve: I'd like to think so. Have I missed anything since this past week?

Erin: No, everyone is either on vacation or going back to school shopping.

Eve: Ok. Keep me posted.

Erin: You keep me posted. Later girl.

As we leave the café, Ben gets a phone call from his elderly neighbor asking if he can help do the yardwork sometime today for him, and the ever-polite Ben agreed. On our walk back, he went straight to his neighbor's house and gave me a key to his house. He assured me he would be back as soon as possible. I let myself in the back door then realized that since is Ben is working, I can sneak out to see Gina without worrying about him looking for me. I call him on my way out, and when he doesn't pick up, I leave a message.

"Hey Ben, it's me. I know you're busy helping next door. I'll call you back in a little while. I'm turning my phone off until then so I can take a nap without interruptions. Of course you're never an interruption. Talk to you later."

Lie. Lie. Lie. It's a lie that won't hurt anyone; that's what I tell myself. I also remind myself that people tell lies to their significant other every day. (Anything as simple as agreeing on your favorite food, not mentioning a study session with another classmate, or even knowing that your partner isn't your first choice. It happens all the time.)

ALTERNATE WORLD

I do know that everyone invited into the alternate world is true to themselves, and that's the way I want to live. I hop back into the routine of walking to the mansion from Boston with my head held high through the double doors. Once in the hallway, I stop to carefully examine every portrait on the wall truly taking in the reason each individual entered this world before me. There are over 200,000 pictures to view. It's not until I'm studying the final picture when Gina comes behind me with a side hug.

"Amazing, isn't it?" She asks.

"You know every person on this wall?" I ask in bewilderment.

"Tapped them all myself."

"Wow! How many years has it been?"

"I don't know. There's no time in the alternate world, but I do know it's been a fulfilling and very long life."

"Will you ever pass on your position?"

"Of course not; I am the keeper of the mansion forever and always."

"So, you outlive everyone who enters here?"

"I wouldn't say outlive. I'd say I'm honored to be surrounded by greatness. Each person on this wall only makes me better. Your picture will be on this wall one day, and I'll say the same about you."

"Thank you, Gina."

"Thank you, Eve. Now to more current events. "How was the wedding back home?"

"How did you know?"

"Oh honey, when are you going to remember I'm fairly all-knowing? I see and hear everything."

"I'm sorry, Gina. I do know that. It was great."

"Did you take your beautiful beau?"

"I did."

"And how was it?"

"Wonderful. I truly believe he was made for me. I had a heart-to-heart with my mom about her choices in life and how we know who to choose as our life partner. She let me in on some secrets from her past I never knew about. I'm realizing that not everyone in a relationship is exactly the same."

"Your mom is a very wise woman."

"I think so. I just don't want to tell her I think that."

Gina chuckles. "Enjoy your evening, dear."

"Thanks. I should be getting back soon."

I take a deep breath as I stare at the portrait of my

great, great grandmother. At least I have someone from my family on my side.

My World:
Chapter Twenty-Seven

When I reach the clearing, the text messages on my phone start coming back in.

Ben: Are you okay? I'm almost done.
Ben: See you in a little while.

I immediately call him, and he answers on the first ring.

Ben: Hey babe. Where are you? I just walked in the house.
Eve: Sorry. I should have called you. I just went out for a run, and I'm coming up the block right now.
Ben: Okay, just glad you're okay. I'm hopping in the shower, but I'll leave the back door open.
Eve: Thanks. See you in a minute.

I'm running up the stairs when I hear the water turn off. I'm in his bedroom by the time he walks in wearing only a brown towel around his waist, that barely covers a thing.

"That's what you went running in?"

I suddenly realize I'm in jeans and a comfy pink off the shoulder top and may be caught in a lie.

"I noticed this morning that I didn't pack a lot of athleisure wear."

"You're not even sweating."

"I actually ended up walking a lot of the way home."

"Well, you look incredible." *He bought it.* He walks confidently over and plants a huge kiss on my mouth before he lets his towel drop.

"Let's order a pizza for dinner," he whispers in my ear. "It's the last night we have together before I lose you to Kerrington Prep." He starts kissing my ear lobe.

"That sounds amazing to me."

He sits up long enough to pick up his cell phone to place a delivery order. In less than two minutes, he's back on top of me and his hands busily move from the top to the bottom part of my torso. I remind him the pizza delivery person is on the way, so we throw our clothes back on and head downstairs to set up a spot to eat. We choose the coffee table in front of the fireplace.

The doorbell rings, so Ben opens the front door to greet and pay the delivery man standing on the front porch. He returns with a large pizza in hand that he puts in the middle of the table. We each take a slice and silently savor the New York style pizza crust. He clears the paper plates and pizza box and leaves them in the kitchen.

"Are you ready for dessert?" Ben asks when he walks back in the den.

"Always!" I excitedly say.

He sits beside me on the sofa and puts a tiny square of chocolate fudge in my mouth. Before I am finished swallowing, he's kissing me all over again. We take turns ripping off each other's clothes and feeling up each other's naked bodies before we fall asleep spooning under a brown wool blanket. When the bright sun shines on our faces, we slowly wake up. Ben throws on his boxers and walks away. He returns about ten minutes later with two bowls of cereal. I wrap myself up in the blanket and sit up beside him to eat.

"Happy first day of school," he jokingly says.

"I know, right. When is your actual first day of classes?"

"Thursday, we all go up to get our schedules and meet our teachers."

"We meet our teachers on Friday. So, your classes start next Monday, too, then?"

"That sounds right."

"Perfect. Let me pack my bag up."

"Take your time. I'll take you back to campus when you're ready."

"Thank you," I say when I kiss him on the cheek before heading upstairs.

I slowly reorganize my luggage, pull my hair up, and

apply some lip gloss. I'm ready to meet Kara and see my old friends and classmates. Ben's waiting at the bottom of the stairs to grab my bag. He makes sure I have everything before he closes and locks the door. He puts my bag in the backseat while I hop in the front seat. Before you know it, we are on campus. He offers to carry my bag to my room, but I tell him I've got it. I'm a second year now. I give Ben a giant hug and soft kiss on the lips before telling him I will see him later this week.

I greet the girls I see when I'm walking up the stairs to the second floor and hug girls in the hall before I unlock my door. When I walk in, Kara is standing on her bed hanging up some pictures. She turns to smile, then hops off the bed.

"Hi Kara, I'm Eve."

"Hi Eve, so nice to meet you," she says when she embraces me.

"Welcome to Kerrington Prep."

"Thank you. Were you here last year?" Kara asks.

"Yes. Where were you?"

"I was in a public high school for my first two years. You were here last year?"

"I was. This was actually my room last year."

"Well, that explains why your side of the room looks so lived in," she laughs.

I laugh and say, "I guess you're right about that."

"Did you have a roommate?"

"I did for the first semester, but it was just me for the rest of the year."

"How was that?"

"It was cool, but I'm excited to have a roommate again."

"Oh good! I'm so glad to have a roommate too."

"Whenever you get settled, we can do dinner together, and I'll introduce you to some of our classmates. Does that sound good?"

"Sounds great!"

I unpack my luggage and rearrange some items in my closet and on my desk until we are both ready to go. Many of our classmates moved in today, but no one really has to be here until Thursday. I'm able to introduce Kara to many of the girls on the hallway, some of the athletes in the dining hall, and give her a basic tour of the campus.

Come Friday, we are ready to get our schedules and reunite with our student body. Kara and I follow thousands of students across the green grass into the gym and look for the second year section amidst the loud cheering and music.

The dean of school gives the annual welcome back speech, then invites the grade level principals to the stage to give the directions and procedures for the rest of the day and the next day. Once we have spent our hours buying books, meeting new teachers, finding our classrooms, and determining our schedule, the weekend is upon us to relax and socialize with friends. I encourage Kara to join me at a baseball player's party off campus where I know Ben will be. He offers to pick us up and take us with him.

I run out to the car, jump in the front seat, and grab Ben's face to smack a kiss on his lips. When Kara gets into the backseat, I introduce the two; Ben turns around to shake her hand and welcome her to Boston. As predicted, the house is so packed, the party guests have overflowed into the yard. Kara and I follow Ben into the house to get a drink then try to find a spot to chat. Kara is wide-eyed watching a couples make out in corners around the house, chugging contests in the back yard, and red solo cups all around the grass. I realize it probably is overwhelming when you're from a small town. I whisper to Ben that we don't want to stay long, and he agrees to take us home as soon as we are ready to go.

Chapter Twenty-Eight

We are all back into the swing of school, which includes the evening and often times weekend study hours. Due to my schedule this year, much of my time during the school week is spent at the library and at my desk. I'm working late one night behind my computer when an email arrives in my mailbox. I click on the sender name, which says Matt Bateman. *You have got to be kidding me!* I open the message, which looks pretty lengthy. I instantly skim over all of the BS about the weather and the subtle hints of his "massive success" in his London internship until I finally decipher the real reason he wrote.

I will be in your neck of the woods tomorrow and was hoping to meet up for coffee. Let me know what time's good for you.

No time is good for me, I think, but deep down I know I could give him at least twenty minutes of time with him since I opted not to continue a relationship with him. I write back a quick reply so as not to mislead the ex-flame.

Hey Matt. I could meet around 11. Does that work for you? We can do that little place near your buddy's home. See you then.

And right before I shut down the computer, I receive a confirming response to 11:00 at "our old spot." *This is going to be interesting.*

The next morning, I actually get to sleep in a bit, until 9:30, before I get up to have some breakfast and mentally prepare for my eleven o'clock appointment. I decide to arrive a little earlier thinking some extra caffeine will do me good. I face the window, enjoying my latte watching the door swing back and forth until the confident six-foot man from my past walks in wearing an obviously very new look. He is dressed to the nines in a polo shirt, blazer, and dark jeans.

"Hi ya, Eve!" Matt shouts, recognizing me instantly.

I stand up to welcome him with a friendly hug.

"Lemme grab some Joe for myself and join you."

Joe? I think, who is the guy? Is this what London boys are like?

"Sounds good," I quietly reply, noticing that Matt is also extremely loud this morning. *Was he always like that?*

A few moments later he is seated across from me,

firing questions.

"How's your second year at Kerrington?"

"It's good. It's much easier the second time around."

"Where are you living?"

"I'm in the same room as I was last year with Jen." I observe his expression change when I mention Jennifer and for a minute, I wonder if he knows more about her relationship than I thought. He then quickly changes the conversation to his favorite topic, himself. He talks about his internship, the details of his flat, and his plans for winter break.

I attempt to be interested but am completely bored out of my mind and very pleased to hear texts dinging on my I-phone. I am even more excited when I notice they are from Ben. I figure that Matt won't even notice if my eyes head south while he describes the hotel he just stayed in on a business meeting in Paris.

Ben: Good morning beautiful. Where are you? I just got back in town with my family and you're the first person I want to see.

Eve: I'm actually at a coffee shop catching up with an old friend. Can't wait to see you later.

Ben: Great, send me the address and I'll see you there.

Eve: You don't have to do that. It's a little off the beaten path near a neighborhood off campus.

Ben: I know exactly. Don't leave!

I mentally rejoin the conversation with Matt to hear he has since moved on to talk about the perks of studying abroad. The time ticks on and I realize I really don't need to be a part of this conversation. There is no conversation. Matt wants a reunion to remind me of how important he is (or he thinks he is). Finally noticing my silence, he looks directly at me.

"You've changed, Eve," he states, staring into my eyes.

"What do you mean?"

"Something is different about you. You haven't said much today."

Not like he has given me more than a minute or two to converse.

"I've just been listening."

"I hear ya."

It is about this moment when Ben walks thru the door; I can't help but light up. He hurries over to the table to give me a kiss on the cheek. I stand up to greet him. He turns to Matt and extends his hand.

"Hi there, I'm Ben. Eve told me she was catching up with an old friend; I hope you don't mind me crashing like this."

Ben turns around to add a chair to the two-person circular table and sits down before Matt responds.

"Not a problem at all. It's nice to meet you. I'm Matt,

Eve's ex-boyfriend."

I turn bright red. "Briefly. This is my first boyfriend from Kerrington Prep I told you about. He's on fall break right now and back in the states."

"I wanted to reconnect with my favorite girlfriend while I am here."

"Ex-boyfriend."

"Tomato, tomahto," Matt snidely responds.

"I see," Ben replies, rather annoyed.

"Don't listen to him, Ben," Eve replies.

"I'm not. I'm not going to sit here and listen to any of this. I'll see you later."

I reach out to pull on his shirt while he stands up to leave, but he doesn't move, and I can't stop him. Once he is fully out of the door, my look of disdain directly hits Matt.

"What the hell was that? What is wrong with you?"

"Seriously, Eve? That guy! We all know he's no good for you."

"Why? Because he's black? You don't even know him."

I hop up to leave shooting daggers one final time at my ex.

"Don't ever contact me again. You have your own life to lead, and I have mine."

I pace to the door of the coffee shop and run down the street toward the tiny parking lot hoping to catch a glimpse of Ben. He's already in his car at the stoplight; I dial his number to see if he will turn around, but he doesn't answer. I call an Uber for a ride to his house. I pray he is home and can see that I only have feelings for him. My driver hits every single red light, so I call him again. Still no answer. Twenty minutes later, I am racing up the stairs and banging on Ben's front door. He answers and closes the door behind him as he stands beside me on the porch. I start in.

"Ben…Ben, I'm so, so sorry." I am panting as I spit out each word. "I don't even know what happened back there."

"Why are you out of breath?" Ben asks just staring at me stoically.

"Maybe because I ran out of the restaurant down the street after you then was panicking my whole ride over here.

"Come in and get some water."

I am silent for a brief few minutes while Ben fills up a glass of water from the faucet and hands it to me. I take a few gulps before talking again."

"Ben, I'm so sorry about Matt. I don't know why he was acting like that."

"I do."

"How do you possibly know?"

"Because I'm a guy. He still has feelings for you."

"No, he doesn't."

"Yes, he does. He's still single, you left him, and now he realizes he never should have let you go and wants you back."

"He didn't say that." Eve's expression shows genuine confusion.

"Of course, he didn't." Ben stays leaning up against the kitchen sink so unnerved then continues. "What happened after I left?"

"I told him to never ever call me again."

"And why did you do that?" Ben stares at me intensely, waiting for a response that I know he wants to hear. This is a scary moment, but I know deep down that this is the time to tell him, so he knows how serious I am about this relationship. I don't want to lose him."

"Because I love you, Ben. I love you. And I only want to be with you."

Ben leans up off the counter to pull me into his chest.

"I love you just the way you are, Eve Thompson, and I have since the day I met you. That will never change."

My heart rate finally slows down. I am feeling truly loved and protected in the arms of my new beau. He gives me a kiss, and I push him away.

"Are your parents here?" I shyly ask.

"No. We came back early because they had a wedding to attend."

"You didn't go?"

"It's someone they work with, but it's close to the

shore, so I know they won't be coming home to this house tonight."

Then he continues kissing me again for most of the day. From the kitchen to the den to the bedroom then back to the den, we catch up on the missed time together since the school year started. I call Kara to tell her I'm staying at Ben's for the night. He and I order dinner and continue to stay immersed in each other's arms until the next morning. The next morning seems very surreal. *This must how you feel when you're with your true love.* I make breakfast for the both of us to enjoy in bed. I tell Ben that I could get used to this moment. Ben just chuckles while he dusts the cinnamon from my face.

"You think that's funny."

"I'm not laughing at what you said. I'm just laughing at you. You're just so cute right now, that's all. I could get used to this moment too."

I kiss Ben once on the lips then finally get up to head back to school.

"Will I see you this week?" Ben hollers while I pace around his bedroom, gathering all of my belongings.

"You mean outside of meeting up for dinner?"

"Well, we can't do this at dinner." He appears directly in front of me, holds my face in his hands, and kisses me slowly.

I'm literally weak in the knees a few minutes before I can speak again.

"Hopefully! I'll call you! I have to catch up with Jen for sure."

"You're going to San Diego this week?"

"No."

"I thought you said you were catching up with Jen?"

And this is it, the deceit. Yes, I know that not all couples tell the truth, but this is a big lie. And why isn't Ben in the alternate world anyway? He is a great guy!

"Oh yea, like on the phone or Zoom or something, I have to schedule some time." *Lie.*

"Okay, well I'll call you later then."

"Sounds great, love you." And I close his bedroom door behind me and let myself out.

When I get back to my room, I call Jen and ask if we can meet sometime this week. She says Tuesday works for her, so it's a date. I begin to make a laundry list of everything I need to talk to Jen about in a few days.

ALTERNATE WORLD

When I arrive at the mansion, I take a seat at the living room bar to order food and check my phone. It doesn't have service, but it does have plenty of photos to review, most from the wedding. Mom and Dad look wonderful. Sam and Hope look so happy. And yes, Ben and I look at peace and in love. That's exactly how I'm feeling. I'm staring at the photo of just Ben and me when Jen gives me a big hug from behind.

Looking over my shoulder, she says, "you two make a beautiful couple." I turn around and give her a big hug.

"Thanks girl. You look beautiful yourself."

"This is what the young mother of a one-year-old looks like."

"I can't believe she's already one!"

"So, you are still with Ben!" She says it so confidently like she knew all long that we are good together.

"I'm still with Ben. And I'm back at Kerrington Prep."

"Do you have a roommate this year?"

"I do. Kara. She's from a small town in Alabama.

226

She's sweet and very quiet. I still miss you though."

"I miss you too. At least we have this place."

"I know. I read recently that the universe slides you love notes in the form of people. You are definitely one of my love notes."

"And you are one of mine. I'm going to get going, but I'm so glad to see your face and glad the wedding was a success. And when I say wedding, I mean you taking Ben home."

I give her a hug and say good-bye before I pick up my phone and bag and head toward the front of the mansion. As I am leaving, Gina gives me a big hug then slinks out of the hallway. As she walks away, I hear her say, "Remember, Eve, people make hard choices every single day. You never know who may show up in the alternate world."

She's exactly right. I remain in the hall a few seconds longer, staring at the front door wondering who may show up next in this world. It could be someone I already know, or it could be a total stranger. It can be a man or woman, girl, or boy, of any age from anywhere in the world. It could be a young man coming out to his religious minister father or a girl who gives up her high society life to take a vow of poverty. You really never know. I know where I am now, I am happy, hopeful, and can truly say I'm living out my dreams. It's not the life I expected, but it's the life I was destined to live. It only happens when we are living our truth.

Twenty-Five Years Later

I am a few months away from my fortieth birthday and believe me when I say I still don't know exactly what the future holds for me in this world, but I do know that Gina was right. Every little decision I made plus a lot of faith along the way has led me to where I am today. Ben and I are happily married, living in Boston, and are both attorneys at his father's high-profile firm that Ben worked for all those years ago. Ben tells people how he loves being married to a famous lawyer (he really has no idea). My parents visit us every fall and visit Hope, her husband, and her baby in London every spring. Christmas in Virginia and family beach vacation in the summer are still annual traditions.

I find that I don't make as many visits to the alternate world as I would like to, but it is the perfect meeting place for Jennifer and me to catch up. She is a successful surgeon, and her daughter is now in medical school. Gina looks exactly the same, always welcoming me with her smile and signature pink. New faces are welcome every single day to the alternate world, but still, no one from my immediate family. I have made my peace with that knowing that we are all responsible for our own choices and decisions. I am fortunate to have my great, great, grandmother with me. I often stare at her portrait with such admiration and pride. I know she's always looking over me in both of my worlds.

I have finally figured out how to balance my real world with my alternate world, and I know that I always have work to do on myself in both. That's called growing up. The comfort is always seeing Gina giving me a goodbye hug and reminding me to continue being my wonderful authentic self. As she told me so many years ago, no matter where I go, as long as I follow my heart and truth, I am always welcome here. And here is exactly where I belong.

The End

About the Author

Kathryn Starke is a national literacy consultant, CEO, reading specialist, author, and former inner-city elementary school teacher. She has previously written books for children, teachers, and Hallmark movie fans. Her very first children's book, *Amy's Travels*, celebrates its 20th anniversary in the summer of 2025. Starke is the creator of the 9th annual Tackle Reading event supported by the National Football League. She founded Creative Minds Publications to help authors bring their books to life.

Connect with Kathryn on Instagram and X @KathrynStarke
Follow @CreativeMindsPublications on Instagram
CreativeMindsPublications.com

Previously Published Books by Kathryn Starke

Amy's Travels

Because of You

Tackle Reading

A Touchdown in Reading: An Educator's Guide to Literacy Instruction

The Perfect Blend

9 798218 516666